THE
CHERRY
ORCHARD

THE
CHERRY
ORCHARD

A Comedy in Four Acts

ANTON CHEKHOV

Translated from the Russian by
Richard Nelson, Richard Pevear
and Larissa Volokhonsky

THEATRE COMMUNICATIONS GROUP
NEW YORK
2015

The Cherry Orchard is published by Theatre Communications Group, Inc., 520 8th Avenue, 24th Floor, New York, NY 10018-4156

The publication of *The Cherry Orchard*, by Richard Nelson, Richard Pevear and Larissa Volokhonsky, through TCG's Book Program, is made possible in part by the New York State Council on the Arts with the support of Governor Andrew Cuomo and the New York State Legislature.

TCG books are exclusively distributed to the book trade by Consortium Book Sales and Distribution.

LIBRARY OF CONGRESS CATALOGING-IN-PUBLICATION DATA
Chekhov, Anton Pavlovich, 1860–1904.
[Vishnevyi sad. English]
The Cherry Orchard : a comedy in four acts / Anton Chekhov ; translated from the Russian by Richard Nelson, Richard Pevear and Larissa Volokhonsky.—
First edition.
pages cm.
(TCG Classic Russian Drama series)
ISBN 978-1-55936-484-3 (paperback)
ISBN 978-1-55936-793-6 (ebook)
I. Nelson, Richard, 1950—translator. II. Pevear, Richard, 1943—translator.
III. Volokhonsky, Larissa, translator. IV. Title.
PG3456.V5V3   2015
891.72'3—dc23   2015009937

Book design and composition by Lisa Govan
Cover design by John Gall

First Edition, July 2015

CONTENTS

INTRODUCTION

The Cherry Orchard, Anton Chekhov's last play, opened at the Moscow Art Theatre on January 17, 1904. The directors of the theater, and of the play, Konstantin Stanislavsky and Vladimir Nemirovich-Danchenko, scheduled the premiere to coincide with Chekhov's forty-fourth name-day (the feast of St. Anthony) and the twenty-fifth anniversary of his entry into literature. At the end of the third act, they brought Chekhov on stage, where he had to endure the applause and congratulations of theater members, critics and the audience—"endure" because Chekhov hated such public attention, and also because the tuberculosis he had suffered from for many years was reaching its final stage and he was barely able to stand through the twenty-minute tribute. Stanislavsky describes the moment in *My Life in Art*: "He stood deathly pale and thin on the right side of the stage and could not control his coughing, while gifts were showered on him and speeches in his honor were being made."*

---

* Konstantin Stanislavsky, *My Life in Art* (Oxford and New York: Routledge, 1987), 422.

He died less than six months later in a sanatorium in Badenweiler, Germany.

Chekhov began to think about writing a new play for the Moscow Art Theatre soon after the production of *Three Sisters* in 1901. In a letter from his home in Yalta to the actress Olga Knipper, whom he was about to marry, he gives some suggestions for their wedding trip, and adds: "At moments I experience an overwhelming desire to write a four-act comedy for the Art Theatre. And I'm going to do so, if nothing interferes, except that I won't let the theater have it before the end of 1903."[†] His facetious calculation of the time turned out to be exact, but his conception of the play as a comedy, which he insisted on, caused disputes that started in his correspondence with Stanislavsky and other members of the Art Theatre even before the play went into rehearsal, and continue to this day.

Stanislavsky and Nemirovich-Danchenko kept urging their leading playwright to give them a new play. On February 5, 1903, Chekhov finally wrote to reassure Stanislavsky: "I do intend to sit down properly with the play after 20 February, and finish it by 20 March. It is all complete in my head. Its title is *The Cherry Orchard*; it has four acts, in the first of which flowering cherry trees are seen through the windows, an entire orchard of white. And the women will be in white dresses."[‡]

However, the work went much more slowly than he anticipated, partly because of his ill health, partly because of the difficulty of the composition itself. In early September, Chekhov wrote to Nemirovich: "My play (if I continue to work as I've been working up to now) will be finished soon, rest assured. Writing the second act was hard, very hard, but it seems to have come out all right." After two further revisions, he mailed the script to Olga Knipper in Moscow. She received it on October 18th. Stanislavsky

---

† Anton Chekhov, *Selected Letters*, ed. by Lillian Hellman (New York: Farrar, Straus and Giroux, 1984), 285.

‡ Rosamund Bartlett, *Anton Chekhov: A Life in Letters* (London: Penguin Books, 2004), 510.

read it the next day and sent Chekhov two enthusiastic telegrams, followed on October 22nd by a passionate letter of appreciation:

> To my mind, *The Cherry Orchard* is your best play. I am fonder of it even than of dear *Seagull*. It is not a comedy nor a farce, as you wrote—it's a tragedy, whatever outlet to a better life you may reveal in the last act. The effect it makes is colossal, achieved by half-tones and delicate pastels . . . I can hear you say: "Excuse me, but it is a farce." . . . No, for the average man it is a tragedy . . . if it were possible, I would really like to play all the parts, darling Charlotta included.[§]

In November, a copy was sent to the theater censors for review. They demanded that two short passages, deemed politically unacceptable, be cut from the speeches of Petya Trofimov in Act Two. In early December Chekhov went to Moscow himself, where he attended rehearsals and made some further small revisions. There his work as playwright ended; the resulting script, with his handwritten corrections, has come down to us. But he also took part in the staging of the play, discussing the sets for each act, the rooms they take place in, the details of the open-air scenery in the second act, the tone and tempo of the production. In late December or early January, however, Stanislavsky insisted on making a major change in the text itself. Chekhov had ended the second act with a hauntingly comic little scene about loss and lostness, set almost in the dark; Stanislavsky wanted instead to end it with Trofimov's bright "premonitions of happiness." He describes the moment in *My Life in Art*:

> . . . when we dared to suggest to Anton Pavlovich that a whole scene be shortened, the whole end of the second act of *The Cherry Orchard*, he became very sad and so

§ Laurence Senelick, *Stanislavsky: A Life in Letters* (London and New York: Routledge, 2013), 167.

pale that we were ourselves frightened at the pain we had caused him. But after thinking for several minutes, he managed to control himself and said:

"All right, shorten it."

Never after did he say a single word to us about this incident. And who knows, perhaps he would have been justified in reproaching us, because it may very well be that it was the will of the stage director and not his own which shortened a scene that was excellently written . . . After the stormy scene with the young people, such a lyric ending lowered the atmosphere of the act and we could not lift it up again. I suppose that it was mainly our own fault, but it was the author who paid for our inability.¶

A new copy of the play, including that revision and some further small changes, was submitted to the censors in January and approved for production. It was published in June 1904 and has remained the standard text for Russian productions and for virtually all the translations and adaptations the play has seen over the past century and more.

. . .

The premiere of *The Cherry Orchard* at the Moscow Art Theatre in 1904 has been called "one of the most influential productions of any play in the history of world theater."** In a recent interview, the British playwright Tom Stoppard, who made an English adaptation of the play, referred to Chekhov as "one of only a handful of people who originated the modern theater."†† But what Chekhov actually produced in *The Cherry Orchard* remains puzzling. Is it a tragedy, a melodrama, a comedy, "in places even a farce,"

¶ Stanislavsky, 418–19.

** James N. Loehlin, *Chekhov: The Cherry Orchard (Plays in Production)* (Cambridge and New York: Cambridge University Press, 2006), 40.

†† Interview with Cathleen McGuigan, *Newsweek*, February 7, 2009.

as Chekhov himself once said? Stanislavsky staged it in a serious naturalistic manner, with an invisible fourth wall, real furniture, windows, drapes, and all sorts of accompanying sounds (birds, farm animals). Vsevolod Meyerhold, who began his career in the Moscow Art Theatre, went on to a more abstract "lyrical-mystic" interpretation of the play under the influence of Russian Symbolism. Soviet productions emphasized the play's historical and political aspects: the inevitable decay of the aristocracy, the foreshadowing of the revolution. There have been nostalgic "upperclass" interpretations, gloomy sentimental interpretations, radical Marxist interpretations, absurdist interpretations, occasionally even "tragi-farcical" interpretations. The running time has varied from ninety minutes to as much as six hours. There are no major theaters in the world that have not staged the play. The history of its adaptations and transformations amounts to a history of twentieth-century theater.

What is it about *The Cherry Orchard* that makes it so compelling and at the same time so elusive? Much of it has to do with Chekhov's innovative composition, its essential indirectness, which implies much more than the words express. This had always been Chekhov's way, in his stories as well as his plays, but in *The Cherry Orchard* it reaches final perfection. What little action there is—the auction of the estate—takes place offstage. The dialogue is not directed by a central conflict or the unfolding of a plot. It is all abrupt shifts, interruptions, non sequiturs; it goes off in different directions, like the bank shots and caroms of Gaev's billiards. A common tendency in productions of the play (and therefore in translations or adaptations) has been to overdetermine the interpretation in one way or another, to confine it to the elegiac, or the political, or the satirical, or the absurd. The essence of Chekhov's art, on the contrary, is inclusion and simultaneity, the rapid shift from one tone to another, the mockery of the most moving moments with slapstick parodies of them—as, for instance, in the series of failed courtships that runs all through the play. The Russian critic Vladimir Kataev wrote in his book on Chekhov: "The principle of permanently changing genre is all-inclusive in *The Cherry Orchard*. Time and again the comic (the limited and relative) is deepened so that we feel sympathy, or, conversely, the serious is brought down to the level of obvious illogicality or repetition."‡‡

These constant shifts require a high degree of attention to detail, from the audience, but first of all from the director and the actors. A good example of what Chekhov expected of them is given in an anecdote from Stanislavsky's *My Life in Art*. Stanislavsky was preparing for the title role in *Uncle Vanya*, whom he conceived as a typical country gentleman and estate manager—a rough-clad horseman wearing tarred boots and a cap and carrying a horsewhip. Chekhov became terribly indignant at that. He said that everything was clearly described in the script and that Stanislavsky must not have read it! Stanislavsky looked through the script, but all he could find was a stage direction for Vanya's first entrance in Act One: "Sits on the bench and straightens his foppish tie."

"Of course," Chekhov explained to him: "Listen, he has a wonderful tie; he is an elegant, cultured man. It's not true that our landed gentry go about in boots smeared with tar. They are wonderful people. They dress well. They order their clothes in Paris. It's all written down."

"This little remark," Stanislavsky adds repentantly, "uncovered the drama of contemporary Russian life."§§

The Cherry Orchard is a fine texture of such revealing details, which give inward dimension and inward movement to people who might otherwise be taken for the stock characters of melodrama. Lopakhin is a case in point. He could be seen, and has sometimes been played, as a typical crude *kulak*, a money-grubbing peasant turned merchant. That is the social stereotype. But Chekhov warned Stanislavsky against it. At the end of October 1903, he wrote:

‡‡ Vladimir Kataev, *If Only We Could Know!*, translated by Harvey Pitcher (Chicago: Ivan R. Dee, 2003), 282.

§§ Stanislavsky, 362.

When I was creating the role of Lopakhin, it was your act-
ing I had in mind ... It is true that Lopakhin is a merchant,
but he is in every sense of the word a decent man; he must
be presented as a wholly dignified, intelligent individual,
not remotely petty or capricious, and it seemed to me that
this role, which is central to the play, would be a brilliant
one for you.¶¶

The complexity of Lopakhin's attitude toward the cherry orchard
itself, if we pay attention to it, reveals the many-sidedness of his
character.

Stanislavsky tended to draw out the production of the play,
to linger over its tender moments, in his elegiac interpretation.
Chekhov wrote in protest to his wife that the fourth act, "which
should last twelve minutes at the most, takes forty minutes in your
production." The high comedy of the play depends, rather, on the
quick succession of its shifts of tone and level. These shifts occur
not only between characters, but within them—most importantly
perhaps in Ranevskaya, who not only owns the cherry orchard but
identifies herself with it. Nemirovich described her as "half Paris,
half cherry orchard," but her character is much richer than his
quip suggests. Chekhov commented to his wife, who first played
the role, "Only death can subdue a woman like that."

Ranevskaya and Lopakhin are both central to the play. Socially
they are opposites, the declining aristocrat and the rising merchant, but Chekhov is interested not in their social differences, but
in the human situation that unites them. He makes that clear from
the very first scene. And the same is true for all the characters. One
thing that unites them is the cherry orchard itself, which is far big-
ger and far more than an ordinary plantation of fruit trees. They all
come rushing into its presence in the first act; in the last act they all
disperse again as the axe begins to fall. Having watched the play, we
are left with all of them, with each of these separate lives, as Chekhov's pitiless but compassionate art has brought them together.

¶¶ Bartlett, 519.

. . .

This edition of *The Cherry Orchard* is unusual in that it includes translations (*not* adaptations) of two complete texts of the play: the script that Chekhov gave to the Moscow Art Theatre in early December 1903, which was his final version; and the script as revised by Stanislavsky and his colleagues for the 1904 premiere, which became the standard version. As we worked on the translation of the standard text, we became interested in what exactly Chekhov had originally given to the theater. We found the differences fascinating and important enough to justify printing full translations of both versions—with the hope that the original 1903 version might finally be staged. Our restoration of the 1903 text was made on the basis of materials published in volume 13 of Chekhov, A. P., *Complete Works and Letters* (Moscow: Academy of Sciences, 1978), 321–334.

In the following note Richard Nelson explains that decision from the point of view of a playwright and director.

—*Richard Pevear*

A NOTE ON THE 1903 SCRIPT

Since its premiere in 1904, every director of every production of *The Cherry Orchard* has been faced with certain questions in the text that need somehow to be addressed. How these questions are addressed has often defined a production's interpretation of this great play.

Here are some of the questions a director of *The Cherry Orchard* has to confront:

- Act One and Act Four have the *same* setting: a room that is "still called the nursery." In Act One this "nursery" appears to be a room that has for years been closed off from the rest of the house (that is, since the death of its last occupant, Ranevskaya's son Grisha). In Act Four *this same room* has somehow become a space that everyone moves through while packing to leave. How does a director (and designer) reconcile this?
- At the beginning of Act One, Lopakhin talks to the maid about an incident from his youth. What makes him

think of this *now*? And why to *the maid*? Or is this just the only way Chekhov could give the audience needed "exposition"?

- When Charlotta is introduced in Act One, she is asked to perform a magic trick, but doesn't want to. Why not? Is she just tired from the journey?

- Anya and Trofimov have often been portrayed in productions as being a young couple in love. Alone at the end of Act One, Trofimov says, "My sunshine! My springtime!" These words have generally been interpreted as referring to Anya. In Act Two, the couple's efforts to get away from the others have been interpreted as the desire of two young lovers to be alone. But if they are in love, why don't they show this love toward each other in Acts Three and Four? Why, in Act Four, isn't their parting more difficult?

- Why doesn't the family *try* to do something to save themselves? Entire productions have been built around answering this question, and by interpreting these characters as being "incapable of doing anything but talk."

- At the top of Act Two, Charlotta confides her "life story" to two uninterested and preoccupied servants. Why to them, and why at this time? Perhaps Charlotta, as I've heard explained, is "just an *eccentric*"?

- In Act Two, Varya, Anya and Trofimov arrive together. Why are they together? Is there any reason why they are together?

As I said, every director has had to ask himself these questions.

But what if the settings of Act One and Act Four were never meant to be the same? What if the family actually does try to do something to help themselves? What if Anya and Trofimov aren't in love? What if Charlotta doesn't confide her life story to two uninterested servants? And so on.

That is, what if, instead of confusions in need of interpretation, these "problems" were simply the result of cuts and changes made, not by the author, but by the director and actors during the course of difficult and volatile rehearsals? What if during such a time, during such rehearsals, changes to the script were made, lines rewritten and rearranged, a setting (Act Four) removed, and so on. And what if nearly every change made was to the detriment of the play?

I believe all that is true, and the following list of the major differences between the two versions will explain why.

A) The location of the setting of Act One and Act Four.

Though the setting for Act One is the same for both versions, in the pre-rehearsal script, the setting for Act Four is *another* room, not the nursery, and most likely an entryway, the same space where the dancing occurs, just offstage, in Act Three. So in Act Four people *do not* walk through the nursery on their way out; therefore the Act One nursery can be designed for what, I believe, is its intention: a room that has been shut off from the rest of the house for years, ever since the death of the son.

This has important consequences for most of the characters, as no one has been in this room for a very long time. And so just entering this nursery must evoke in each of them lost or repressed wounds and memories.

As the play opens, Lopakhin follows the maid, Dunyasha, into this room, probably after having heard the train whistle. He follows her in to ask a question and only *then* realizes where he is—in a forgotten inner sanctum. Memories pour out of Lopakhin, all related to this room. In the pre-rehearsal version, Lopakhin last visited here when he was "five or six." In the later, post-rehearsal text, he last visited when he was "fifteen." The greater the distance, of course, the greater the jolt to his memory, which helps explain why these memories seem to suddenly pour out.

So Lopakhin, with memories overwhelming him, doesn't actually talk to the maid, but rather to himself, and, perhaps, to this room where he once found refuge so many years ago, as a young boy, and was treated so well by a girl.

Anya calls from offstage, "Let's go through here." So it is clear that this nursery is not the "direct" route to where they are headed, but rather a detour. This room has been opened up *for a purpose.* One could even say that here is the underlying "plot" of the entire first act—everyone dealing with this room, and the memories and ghosts it evokes.

Gaev's "bookcase speech" then is not some random memory of a man who has random bursts of nostalgia, as it is often played. It is much more immediate and about an event that has recently occurred. He explains that just "last week" he pulled out the lower drawer. It seems, then, that they opened up this room *only* last week, no doubt in preparation for Lyubov Andreevna's return. So this room is new for everyone.

One begins to sense that after all these years since the boy's death, the family is now ready to try and deal with this nursery and its memories, wounds and guilt.

Trofimov enters. Why is he here? There is no suggestion in the play that he has come often *or* has ever been back since the boy in his charge accidentally drowned. It is even possible that this is his first time back. In any event, as the nursery has been closed off, he too has not been in this room for years; this room where he spent his youth, before the death of his charge and before the guilt that that would have brought him. A guilt that he now carries with him and constantly brings up, in different ways, throughout the rest of the play.

So at the end of Act One, when Trofimov, alone, says tenderly, "My sunshine. My springtime," isn't he referring to the eleven-year-old Anya, to this nursery, to the lost child, and to his own lost youth? Instead of the beginnings of a love affair that never evolves in the play, perhaps these last two words are the *cri de coeur* of a man wracked with a guilt evoked by all the associations he has with this room.

Knowing that this setting is unique to Act One, and will not need to also function as a passageway in Act Four, should free a director and designer to investigate the emotional weight of this room, and how the nursery acts as a catalyst for the play as a whole.

B) Charlotta and her magic.

In the 1903 text, unlike the post-rehearsal text, Charlotta does do a magic trick when she enters in Act One. This may seem like an unimportant difference; however, given the number of changes made to Charlotta's character in the post-rehearsal text, the restitution of this trick goes a long way to clarifying Charlotta's role in the play as a whole.

Her magic trick in Act One is to go to a door, and somehow create a "knocking" on this door from the outside. She then "asks" who it is. And so explains to the others—"this is my gentleman fiancé." In other words, she implies—with a sort of wink—that this fiancé is but a figment of her imagination; he doesn't exist, and will never appear.

Varya is right there in the room, and Varya (at somewhat greater length in the 1903 version) has just talked about waiting for Lopakhin to propose. So Charlotta, from her first entrance, via her "ventriloquism," takes on the role of saying what everyone else knows to be true but dares not say—that Varya's waiting for Lopakhin is perhaps in vain. In other words, from her entrance, she is very much like a Shakespearean fool, and this will be her role throughout the play.

C) What happens between Acts One and Two and other changes in Act Two.

Most of the changes made during the Moscow Art rehearsals occurred in Act Two. In the 1903 version, Act Two opens not with Charlotta talking to preoccupied servants about her life, but with Anya and Trofimov passing by Dunyasha, Epikhodov and Yasha in the field. Anya has just returned from three weeks at her great-aunt's, where she went to ask for financial help.

Right away we discover that the family has indeed made an effort to save the estate; they have, in fact, tried to put into motion one of the plans Gaev thought up in Act One. So perhaps they are not as blind to their situation as has often been assumed.

Trofimov and Anya notice they are not alone and so head down to the riverbank. With Anya having been away for three weeks, they have hardly had a chance to talk since Act One. Anya, we later learn, wants to know all about life in the real world, as that is where she has decided she is headed (and by the end of Act Four that is where she goes). The two have so many things to share—about loss and guilt and fear; but nowhere is there talk of love for each other. Varya is the only person who suggests this; the same Varya who has marriage and fiancés on her mind from the beginning of the play to the very end.

In the 1903 script, Varya and Charlotta pass by. Varya is suspicious and is looking for Anya and Trofimov. She suspects a love affair. She notices the young couple on the bank of the river. Charlotta seems to be going hunting with gun in tow, and perhaps has only just bumped into Varya. Varya, having spied the young couple, hurries after them. Charlotta wanders off.

A while later, in both versions, Varya returns with Anya and Trofimov. Because of the earlier scene, we now know that Varya found the couple, and has dragged them back from the river, as their self-appointed chaperone. Knowing this creates a rich chemistry between them for the rest of the scene.

The next and perhaps most significant difference between the versions occurs at the end of the act. There is an entirely new scene in the 1903 text:

Firs returns to an empty and nearly dark stage. Charlotta wanders in and notices him. Charlotta and Firs sit together on the bench. Firs explains that his mistress has lost her purse. Charlotta replies that the mistress "constantly loses things. She's lost her life, too." And it is *this* thought that gets her to tell her own "life story" to *Firs* (rather than to two uninterested servants).

Firs then talks about a time in his youth when he was sent to jail. He goes on to tell a story about when he was a boy and was with his father on a wagon full of sacks. He noticed that inside one sack there was another sack, and in that other sack something went "wiggle-wiggle." That makes Charlotta laugh (as she eats her cucumber). And with Varya's voice from off calling, "Anya! Where are you?" this scene, worthy of Samuel Beckett, ends.

In his autobiography, *My Life in Art* (Routledge, 1987), Stanislavsky writes that he just couldn't make the scene work and adds: "I suppose that it was mainly our own fault, but it was the author who paid for our inability." What was lost as a result was perhaps the most subtle and seemingly inconsequential expression of Chekhov's central concern in the play.

In our translation of the 1903 script, the changes made by Stanislavsky during rehearsals have been eliminated,*** and the cuts have been restored.

—Richard Nelson

*** With one small exception. In Act Four, Trofimov comments on Lopakhin's hands: "I still like you. You have fine, delicate fingers, like an artist . . ." This was an addition made during the rehearsals. It is clear from his letters that Chekhov was concerned that Lopakhin not be portrayed as a coarse peasant. He added this description after the naturally elegant Stanislavsky, for whom he conceived the role, had turned it down (he played Gaev instead). The detail is as telling as Uncle Vanya's foppish tie.

THE CHERRY ORCHARD

1903 Script

Characters

LYUBÓV ANDRÉEVNA RANÉVSKAYA (Lyúba), a landowner

ÁNYA (Ánechka), her daughter, seventeen years old

VÁRYA (Varvára Mikháilovna), her adopted daughter, twenty-four years old

LEONÍD ANDRÉEVICH GÁEV (Lyónya), Ranevskaya's brother

ERMOLÁI ALEXÉEVICH LOPÁKHIN (Alexéich), a merchant

PYÓTR SERGÉEVICH TROFÍMOV (Pétya), a student

BORÍS BORÍSOVICH SIMEÓNOV-PÍSHCHIK, a landowner

CHARLÓTTA IVÁNOVNA [no last name], a governess

SEMYÓN PANTELÉEVICH EPIKHÓDOV, a clerk

DUNYÁSHA (Avdótya Fyódorvna Kozoédova), a maid

FIRS (Nikolaevich), a servant, eighty-seven years old

YÁSHA, a young servant

A PASSERBY

THE STATIONMASTER

A POSTAL CLERK

GUESTS, SERVANTS

The action takes place on L. A. Ranevskaya's estate.

ACT ONE

A room which is still called the nursery. One of the doors leads to Anya's room. Daybreak, the sun will rise soon. It is already May, the cherry trees are in bloom, but it is chilly. There is a morning frost in the orchard. The windows in the room are shut.

Dunyasha enters with a candle and Lopakhin with a book in his hand.

LOPAKHIN

The train's come, thank God. What time is it?

DUNYASHA

Going on two. *(Blows out the candle)* It's already light.

LOPAKHIN

How late does that make the train? A couple of hours at least. *(Yawns and stretches)* I'm a fine one, too! Made a fool of myself! Came here on purpose to meet them at the station, and slept right through it . . . Sat down and fell asleep. A shame . . . You might have waked me up.

3

DUNYASHA

I thought you left. *(Listens)* There, I think it's them.

LOPAKHIN

(Listens) No . . . They've got to pick up the luggage and all that . . .

Pause.

Lyubov Andreevna's been living abroad for five years. I don't know what she's like now . . . She's a good person. Easy, simple. I remember when I was a kid of about five or six, my late father—he kept a shop then, here in the village—punched me in the face with his fist. My nose bled . . . We had come here to the yard together for some reason, and he was a bit drunk. Lyubov Andreevna, I remember it like today, still a young thing, so slender, she led me to the washstand, here, in this same room, in the nursery. "Don't cry, peasant-boy," she says, "it'll go away by your wedding day . . ."

Pause.

Peasant-boy . . . True, my father was a peasant, but here I am in a white waistcoat and yellow shoes. A pig in the parlor. Oh, I'm rich all right, I've got lots of money, but if you really look into it, I'm as peasant as a peasant can be . . . *(Leafs through the book)* I'm reading this book and don't understand a thing. I fell asleep reading it.

Pause.

DUNYASHA

And the dogs didn't sleep all night. They can sense the masters are coming.

LOPAKHIN

Dunyasha, why are you so—

DUNYASHA

My hands are trembling.

LOPAKHIN

You're much too pampered, Dunyasha. You dress like a young lady, and do your hair up, too. It's not right. Remember who you are.

Epikhodov enters with a bouquet. He wears a jacket and brightly polished boots that creak loudly. He drops the bouquet as he enters.

EPIKHODOV

(Picking up the bouquet) The gardener sent it. He says to put it in the dining room. *(He hands the bouquet to Dunyasha)*

LOPAKHIN

And bring me some kvass.

DUNYASHA

Yes, sir. *(Exits)*

EPIKHODOV

There's a morning frost, three below, and the cherry trees are all in bloom. I cannot approve of our climate. *(He sighs)* I cannot. Our climate cannot aptly contribute. And allow me to append another thing, Ermolai Alexeich. I bought myself some boots two days ago, and, I venture to assure you, they creak so much it's quite impossible. Can I grease them with something?

LOPAKHIN

Leave me alone. I'm sick of you.

EPIKHODOV

Every day some new catastrophe befalls me. And I don't complain, I'm used to it, I even smile.

Dunyasha enters, serves Lopakhin his kvass.

I'm leaving. *(He bumps into a chair, which falls over)* There . . . *(As if triumphantly)* There, you see. What a happenstance, by the way, if you'll pardon the expression . . . It's simply even remarkable! *(Exits)*

5

DUNYASHA

And I must tell you, Ermolai Alexeich, Epikhodov has proposed to me.

LOPAKHIN

Ah!

DUNYASHA

I really don't know how to . . . He's nice enough, only sometimes he gets to talking so you don't understand a thing. It's good, it's got feeling, only it's incomprehensible. I even seem to like him. He's an unlucky man, every day there's something. They tease him about it here, they call him "Two-and-twenty Catastrophes."

LOPAKHIN

(Listens) There, I think it's them . . .

DUNYASHA

It's them! What's the matter with me . . . I've gone cold all over.

LOPAKHIN

It's really them. Let's go and meet them. Will she recognize me? Five years we haven't seen each other.

DUNYASHA

(Agitated) Lord . . . Lord . . .

The sound of two carriages driving up to the house. Lopakhin and Dunyasha exit quickly. The stage is empty. Noise starts in the adjacent rooms. Firs, who went to meet Lyubov Andreevna, hastily crosses the stage, leaning on a stick; he is wearing old-fashioned livery and a top hat. He says something to himself, but it is impossible to make out a single word. The noise backstage keeps growing louder. A voice says: "Let's go through here . . ." Lyubov Andreevna, Anya and Charlotta Ivanovna with a little dog on a leash enter, dressed in traveling clothes. They are followed by Varya, wearing

*a coat and shawl, Gaev, Simeonov-Pishchik, Lopakhin, Dunyasha
with a bundle and an umbrella, servants with the luggage. They all
walk through the room.*

ANYA

Let's go through here. Do you remember what room this is, mama?

LYUBOV ANDREEVNA

(Joyfully, through tears) The nursery!

VARYA

It's so cold! My hands are freezing. *(To Lyubov Andreevna)* Your
rooms, the white one and the violet one, have stayed just as they
were, mama.

LYUBOV ANDREEVNA

The nursery, my dear, beautiful room . . . I slept here when I was
little . . . *(Weeps)* And it's as if I'm little now . . . *(She kisses her
brother, then Varya, then her brother again)* And Varya's the same
as before, looking like a nun. And I recognize Dunyasha . . . *(She
kisses Dunyasha)*

GAEV

The train was two hours late. How about that, eh? How about that
for efficiency?

CHARLOTTA

(To Pishchik) My dog eats nuts also.

PISHCHIK

(Surprised) Imagine that!

Exit all but Anya and Dunyasha

DUNYASHA

How we waited . . . *(She takes Anya's coat and hat)*

ANYA

I didn't sleep for four nights on the train . . . I'm so chilled now.

DUNYASHA

You left during the Great Lent, there was snow then, it was freezing, and now? My dear! *(Laughs, kisses her)* How I waited for you, my joy, my angel . . . I'll tell you now, I can't wait . . .

ANYA

(Listlessly) Here we go again . . .

DUNYASHA

The clerk Epikhodov proposed to me after Easter.

ANYA

That's all you ever . . . *(Straightens her hair)* I lost all my hairpins . . . *(She is very tired, even staggers a little)*

DUNYASHA

I just don't know what to think. He loves me, he loves me so!

ANYA

(Looks through the door to her room, tenderly) My room, my windows, as if I never left. I'm home! Tomorrow morning I'll get up and run out to the orchard . . . Oh, if only I could fall asleep! I didn't sleep all the way, I was worn out with worry.

DUNYASHA

Pyotr Sergeich arrived two days ago.

ANYA

(Joyfully) Petya!

DUNYASHA

He's asleep in the bathhouse. That's where he's staying. I'm afraid to inconvenience them, he says. *(Glancing at her pocket watch)*

I ought to wake him up, but Varvara Mikhailovna told me not to. Don't wake him up, she says.

Varya enters with a bunch of keys hanging from her belt.

VARYA

Dunyasha, coffee, quickly . . . Mama's asking for coffee.

DUNYASHA

Right away. *(Exits)*

VARYA

Well, thank God you've come. You're home again. *(Caressingly)* My darling has come! My beauty has come!

ANYA

I've been through a lot.

VARYA

I can imagine!

ANYA

I left during Holy Week. It was cold then. Charlotta talked all the way, and played card tricks. Why on earth did you stick me with Charlotta . . .

VARYA

You couldn't have gone alone, darling. Not at seventeen!

ANYA

We arrive in Paris. It's cold there, snowy. My French is awful. Mama lives on the fifth floor, I go in, there are some French people there, ladies, an old padre with a book, cigarette smoke, cheerless. I suddenly felt so sorry for mama, so sorry, I took her head in my arms, pressed it to me, and couldn't let go. After that mama just kept hugging me and crying . . .

VARYA

(Through tears) Don't tell me, don't . . .

ANYA

She had already sold her house near Menton, and she had nothing left, nothing. I also didn't have a kopeck left, we barely made it home. And mama doesn't understand! We sit down to dinner in the station and she orders the most expensive things and tips the waiter a rouble. Then there's Charlotta. Yasha also orders something. It's just awful. Mama has this servant Yasha, we've brought him with us . . .

VARYA

I saw the scoundrel.

ANYA

Well, so, how are things? Have we paid the interest?

VARYA

Far from it.

ANYA

My God, my God . . .

VARYA

They'll put the estate up for sale in August . . .

ANYA

My God . . .

LOPAKHIN

(Peeks through the door and moos) Meu-u-h. *(Exits)*

VARYA

(Through tears) Oh, I could give it to him . . . *(Shakes her fist)*

ANYA

(Embraces Varya) Varya, has he proposed? *(Varya shakes her head no)* But he does love you . . . Why don't you have a talk? What are you waiting for?

VARYA

I don't think it'll come to anything. He has a lot to do, he can't be bothered with me . . . he pays no attention. Enough of him, it's hard for me to look at him . . . Everybody talks about us getting married, everybody congratulates me, and he himself looks like he's just about to propose, but in fact there's nothing, it's all like a dream, a troubling, bad dream . . . Sometimes I'm even frightened. I don't know what to do with myself . . . *(In a different tone)* Your brooch looks like a little bee.

ANYA

(Sadly) Mama bought it for me. *(Goes to her room, talks gaily, childishly)* In Paris I flew in a hot-air balloon.

VARYA

My darling's come home! My beauty's come home!

Dunyasha has now returned with the coffee pot and is preparing coffee.

(Standing by the door) I go around all day, darling, looking after the house, and I keep dreaming. To see you married to a rich man. I'd be at peace then, and I'd take myself to a convent, then to Kiev . . . to Moscow, and go around like that to all the holy places . . . go on and on. What blessedness!

ANYA

The birds are singing in the orchard. What time is it?

VARYA

Must be nearly three. It's time you went to bed, darling. *(Going into Anya's room)* What blessedness!

11

ANTON CHEKHOV

Yasha enters with a lap blanket and a traveling bag.

YASHA

(Walks across the stage) May I pass through here?

DUNYASHA

I'd never have recognized you, Yasha. See what's become of you abroad!

YASHA

Hm . . . And who are you?

DUNYASHA

I was only so high when you left . . . *(Shows height from the floor)* Dunyasha, Fyodor Kozoedov's daughter. Don't you remember?!

YASHA

Hm . . . A cute little cucumber! *(Glances around and embraces her; she cries out and drops a saucer. Yasha quickly exits)*

VARYA

(In the doorway, displeased) What's going on here?

DUNYASHA

(Through tears) I broke a saucer . . .

VARYA

That means good luck.

ANYA

(Coming out of her room) We should warn mama that Petya's here . . .

VARYA

I gave orders not to wake him up.

ANYA

(Pensively) Father died six years ago. A month later my brother Grisha drowned in the river—a seven-year-old boy. Mama couldn't

bear it, she left, left without looking back . . . *(Shudders)* How well I understand her, if only she knew!

Pause.

And Petya Trofimov was Grisha's tutor, he might remind her of . . .

Firs enters wearing a jacket and white waistcoat.

FIRS

(Approaches the coffee pot, preoccupied) The lady will have coffee here . . . *(Puts on white gloves)* Is the coffee ready? *(Sternly, to Dunyasha)* You! Where's the cream?

DUNYASHA

Oh, my God . . . *(Exits quickly)*

FIRS

(Fussing over the coffee pot) Eh, you blunderhead . . . *(Mutters to himself)* So they're home from Paris . . . Used to be the master went to Paris . . . by horse and carriage . . . *(Laughs)*

VARYA

What is it, Firs?

FIRS

If you please. *(Joyfully)* My lady has come home! How I've waited! Now I can die . . . *(Weeps from joy)*

VARYA

You foolish man.

Lyubov Andreevna, Gaev, Lopakhin and Simeonov-Pishchik enter. Simeonov-Pishchik is wearing a sleeveless jacket of fine broadcloth and balloon trousers.
    Gaev, as he enters, makes the motions of playing billiards.

LYUBOV ANDREEVNA

How does it go? Let me remember . . . Yellow into the corner! Double into the side!

GAEV

Cut shot into the corner! Once upon a time you and I slept in this room, sister, and now I'm already fifty-one, strangely enough . . .

LOPAKHIN

Yes, time flies.

GAEV

Whoso?

LOPAKHIN

I said, time flies.

GAEV

It smells of cheap cologne here.

ANYA

I'm going to bed. Good night, mama. *(Kisses her mother)*

LYUBOV ANDREEVNA

My beloved little baby. *(Kisses her hands)* Are you glad to be home? I can't get over it.

ANYA

Good-bye, uncle.

GAEV

(Kisses her face and hands) God bless you. You're so much like your mother! *(To his sister)* You were exactly the same at her age, Lyuba.

Anya gives her hand to Lopakhin and Pishchik, exits, and closes the door behind her.

LYUBOV ANDREEVNA

She's very tired.

PISHCHIK

It must have been a long trip.

VARYA

(To Lopakhin and Pishchik) Well, gentlemen? It's nearly three, don't wear out your welcome.

LYUBOV ANDREEVNA

(Laughs) You're still the same, Varya. *(Pulls her to herself and kisses her)* I'll have my coffee, then we'll all go.

Firs puts a little cushion under her feet.

Thank you, dearest. I've gotten used to coffee. I drink it day and night. Thank you, my dear old man. *(She kisses Firs)*

VARYA

I'll see if they've brought all the things . . . *(Exits)*

LYUBOV ANDREEVNA

Can it be me sitting here? *(Laughs)* I want to jump around, wave my arms. *(Covers her face with her hands)* What if I'm asleep! God is my witness, I love my country, love it tenderly, I couldn't look out of the train, I kept crying. *(Through tears)* I must have my coffee, though. Thank you, Firs, thank you, my dear old man. I'm so glad you're still alive.

FIRS

Two days ago.

GAEV

He's hard of hearing.

15

LOPAKHIN

I've got to leave for Kharkov at five this morning. What a shame! I wanted to have a look at you, to talk a little . . . You're as magnificent as ever.

PISHCHIK

Even got prettier . . . Dressed up Parisian-style . . . really bowls me over . . .

LOPAKHIN

Your brother, Leonid Andreevich here, goes around saying I'm a boor, a money-grubber, but it's decidedly all the same to me. Let him talk. All I want is for you to believe me like before, that your astonishing, moving eyes look at me like before. Merciful God! My father was your grandfather's serf, and your father's, but you, you personally, once did so much for me that I've forgotten all that and love you like one of my own . . . more than one of my own.

LYUBOV ANDREEVNA

I can't sit still, I just can't . . . *(Jumps up and paces about in great excitement)* I won't survive this joy . . . Laugh at me, I'm stupid . . . My own little bookcase . . . *(Kisses the bookcase)* My little table.

GAEV

Nanny died while you were away.

LYUBOV ANDREEVNA

(Sits down and drinks her coffee) Yes, God rest her soul. They wrote to me.

GAEV

And Anastasy died. Cross-eyed Petrushka left me and now lives in town at the police chief's. *(Takes a box of fruit drops from his pocket, sucks on one)*

PISHCHIK

My daughter, Dashenka . . . sends you her greetings . . .

LOPAKHIN

I would like to tell you something very pleasant and cheerful. *(Looks at his watch)* I've got to go now, there's no time to talk . . . well, so, in two or three words. As you already know, your cherry orchard is going to be sold off to pay your debts, the auction will be on August twenty-second, but don't worry, rest easy, there's a way out . . . Here's my plan. Please pay attention! Your estate is located only fifteen miles from town, the railroad now passes nearby, and if the cherry orchard and the land by the river were broken up into lots and leased out for building summer houses, you'd have an income of at least twenty-five thousand a year.

GAEV

Excuse me, but that's nonsense!

LYUBOV ANDREEVNA

I don't quite understand you, Ermolai Alexeich.

LOPAKHIN

You'll charge the summer people a yearly rent of at least ten roubles per acre, and if you advertise right now, I'll bet anything you like that by autumn you won't have a single free scrap left, it'll all be snapped up. In short, congratulations, you're saved. The location's wonderful, the river's deep. Though, of course, there'll have to be some clearing away, some cleaning up . . . for instance, you'll have to pull down all the old buildings, like this house, which is no longer good for anything, and chop down the old cherry orchard . . .

LYUBOV ANDREEVNA

Chop it down? My dear, forgive me, but you understand nothing. If there's one thing in the whole province that's interesting, even remarkable, it's our cherry orchard.

LOPAKHIN

The only remarkable thing about this orchard is that it's very big. It produces cherries once in two years, and there's nothing to do with them, nobody buys them.

GAEV

This orchard is even mentioned in the *Encyclopedia*.

LOPAKHIN

(Glancing at his watch) If we don't come up with anything and don't reach any decision, both the cherry orchard and the entire estate will be sold at auction on August twenty-second. Make up your minds! There's no other way out, I swear to you. None. None.

FIRS

In the old days, forty or fifty years ago, the cherries were dried, bottled, made into juice, preserves, and we used to . . .

GAEV

Be quiet, Firs.

FIRS

And we used to send cartloads of dried cherries to Moscow and Kharkov. The money we made! And those dried cherries were soft, juicy, sweet, fragrant . . . They knew a way . . .

LYUBOV ANDREEVNA

And where is that way now?

FIRS

Forgotten. Nobody remembers it.

PISHCHIK

(To Lyubov Andreevna) How are things in Paris? Eh? Eat any frogs?

LYUBOV ANDREEVNA

No . . . crocodiles.

PISHCHIK

Imagine that . . .

LOPAKHIN

Before there were just gentry and peasants here, but now these summer people have appeared. All the towns, even the smallest ones, are surrounded by summer houses now. And it's safe to say that in some ten or twenty years the summer people will multiply and begin to work. Right now they only drink tea on their balconies, but it may well happen that they take to farming their little acres, and then your cherry orchard will become happy, rich . . .

GAEV

(Indignantly) What nonsense!

Varya and Yasha enter.

VARYA

Two telegrams came for you, mama. *(Chooses a key and with a ringing noise opens the old bookcase)* Here they are.

LYUBOV ANDREEVNA

From Paris. *(Tears up the telegrams without reading them)* I'm through with Paris . . .

GAEV

Do you know how old this bookcase is, Lyuba? Last week I pulled out the lower drawer, I look, there are numbers burnt into it. This bookcase was made exactly a hundred years ago. How about that? Eh? We could celebrate its jubilee. It's an inanimate object, but still, all the same, it's a bookcase.

PISHCHIK

(Surprised) A hundred years . . . Imagine that . . .

GAEV

Yes . . . That's something . . . *(Pats the bookcase)* Dear, much-esteemed bookcase! I hail your existence, which for more than a hundred years now has been intent upon the bright ideals of justice and the good.

19

Your silent summons to fruitful work has never slackened in those hundred years, maintaining courage in the generations of our family, *(He becomes tearful)* faith in a better future, and fostering in us the ideals of the good and of social consciousness.

Pause.

LOPAKHIN

Hm, yes . . .

LYUBOV ANDREEVNA

You're the same as ever, Lyonya.

GAEV

(Slightly embarrassed) Carom into the right corner! Cut shot into the side!

LOPAKHIN

(Glancing at his watch) Well, time to go.

YASHA

(Offering Lyubov Andreevna medicine) Maybe you'll take your pills now . . .

PISHCHIK

No need to take medicines, my dear . . . they do no harm, and no good . . . Let me have them . . . my most respected lady. *(Takes the pills, pours them into his palm, blows on them, puts them in his mouth, and washes them down with kvass)* There!

LYUBOV ANDREEVNA

(Frightened) You're out of your mind!

PISHCHIK

I took all the pills.

LOPAKHIN

A bottomless pit.

Everybody laughs.

FIRS

The gentleman came here during Holy Week and ate half a bucket of pickles . . . *(Mutters something)*

LYUBOV ANDREEVNA

What's he saying?

VARYA

He's been muttering like that for three years now. We're used to it.

YASHA

On the decline.

Charlotta Ivanovna, in a white dress, very thin, tightly corseted, with a lorgnette at her waist, walks across the stage.

LOPAKHIN

Forgive me, Charlotta Ivanovna, I haven't greeted you yet. *(Tries to kiss her hand)*

CHARLOTTA

(Pulling her hand back) If I allow you to kiss my hand, then you'll want to kiss my elbow, then my shoulder . . .

LOPAKHIN

I have no luck today.

Everybody laughs.

Charlotta Ivanovna, show us a trick.

LYUBOV ANDREEVNA

Show us a trick, Charlotta!

CHARLOTTA

(Going to the door) Someone is standing behind the door. Who's there? *(Knocking on the door from the other side)* Who's knocking? *(More knocking)* This is my gentleman fiancé. *(Exits)*

Everybody laughs.

LOPAKHIN

See you in three weeks. *(Kisses Lyubov Andreevna's hand)* Good-bye for now. It's time. *(To Gaev)* Bye-bye. *(Exchanges kisses with Pishchik)* Bye-bye. *(Gives his hand to Varya, then to Firs and Yasha)* I don't feel like leaving. *(To Lyubov Andreevna)* Think it over about the summer houses, and if you decide to do it, let me know. I'll get you a loan of fifty thousand. Think seriously.

VARYA

(Angrily) Will you finally leave?!

LOPAKHIN

I'm leaving, I'm leaving . . . *(Exits)*

GAEV

A boor. *Pardon*, however . . . Varya's going to marry him, he's Varya's little suitor.

VARYA

You talk too much, uncle dear.

LYUBOV ANDREEVNA

Why, Varya, I'll be very glad. He's a good man.

PISHCHIK

A most worthy man . . . to tell the truth . . . And my Dashenka . . . also says . . . says various things. *(Snores, then wakes up at once)* Anyhow, my most respected lady, lend me two hundred and forty roubles . . . to pay my mortgage interest tomorrow . . .

VARYA

(Frightened) We can't, we can't!

LYUBOV ANDREEVNA

I really have nothing at all.

PISHCHIK

It'll turn up. *(Laughs)* I never lose hope. That's it, I think, all is lost, I'm ruined, but, lo and behold—they build the railroad across my land, and . . . they pay me for it. Then, lo and behold, something else comes along, if not today then tomorrow . . . Dashenka wins two hundred thousand . . . on a lottery ticket.

LYUBOV ANDREEVNA

We've had our coffee, we can retire.

FIRS

(Brushing Gaev off, admonishingly) Again you've put on the wrong trousers. What am I to do with you!

VARYA

(Softly) Anya's asleep. *(Quietly opens the window)* The sun's up, it's not cold anymore. Look, mama: what wonderful trees! My God, what air! The starlings are singing!

GAEV

(Opens the other window) The orchard's all white. You haven't forgotten, Lyuba? That long alley goes straight on, straight on, like a belt stretched out. It glistens on moonlit nights. You remember? You haven't forgotten?

LYUBOV ANDREEVNA

(Looks out the window at the orchard) Oh, my childhood, my purity! I slept in this nursery, looked out from here at the orchard, happiness woke up with me every morning, and it was the same then as it is now, nothing has changed. *(Laughs joyfully)* All, all

white! Oh, my orchard! After dark, rainy autumn and cold winter, you are young again, full of happiness, the angels of heaven have not abandoned you . . . If only the heavy stone could be lifted from my breast and shoulders, if only I could forget my past!

GAEV

Yes, and the orchard's going to be sold to pay our debts, strangely enough . . .

LYUBOV ANDREEVNA

Look, my late mother is walking through the orchard . . . in a white dress! *(Laughs joyfully)* It's her!

GAEV

Where?

VARYA

God help you, mama.

LYUBOV ANDREEVNA

No, there's nobody, I imagined it. To the right, at the turn towards the gazebo, there's a little white tree bending down . . . It looks like a woman . . .

Trofimov enters in a shabby student uniform, wearing glasses.

What an amazing orchard! Masses of white flowers, the blue sky . . .

TROFIMOV

Lyubov Andreevna!

She turns to look at him.

I'll just say hello and leave at once. *(Kisses her hand warmly)* I was told to wait till morning, but I got impatient . . .

Lyubov Andreevna looks at him, perplexed.

VARYA

(Through tears) It's Petya Trofimov . . .

TROFIMOV

Petya Trofimov, former tutor of your Grisha . . . Can I have changed so much?

Lyubov Andreevna embraces him and weeps quietly.

GAEV

(Embarrassed) Enough, enough now, Lyuba.

VARYA

(Weeps) I told you to wait till tomorrow, Petya.

LYUBOV ANDREEVNA

My Grisha . . . my little boy . . . Grisha . . . my son . . .

VARYA

There's no help for it, mama. It was God's will.

TROFIMOV

(Gently, through tears) There, there . . .

LYUBOV ANDREEVNA

(Weeps softly) My little boy died, he drowned . . . Why? Why, my friend? *(More softly)* Anya's asleep in there, and I talk so loudly . . . make noise . . . Well, so, Petya? How is it you've lost your looks? How is it you've aged so much?

TROFIMOV

A peasant woman on the train once called me a mangy mister.

LYUBOV ANDREEVNA

You were still a boy then, a sweet young student, and now—thin hair, glasses. Can it be you're still a student? *(Goes toward the door)*

TROFIMOV

Must be I'm an eternal student.

LYUBOV ANDREEVNA

(Kisses her brother, then Varya) Well, go to bed . . . You've aged, too, Leonid.

PISHCHIK

(Follows her) So, it's to bed now . . . Ah, this gout of mine. I'll stay here . . . Lyubov Andreevna, my dear heart, maybe, tomorrow morning . . . two hundred and forty roubles . . .

GAEV

He's still at it.

PISHCHIK

Two hundred and forty roubles . . . to pay the interest on the mortgage.

LYUBOV ANDREEVNA

I have no money, dear heart.

PISHCHIK

I'll pay it back, my dear . . . It's nothing . . .

LYUBOV ANDREEVNA

Well, all right, Leonid will give it to you . . . Give it to him, Leonid.

GAEV

Give it to him, hah! Good luck!

LYUBOV ANDREEVNA

What can we do? Give it to him . . . He needs it . . . He'll pay it back.

Lyubov Andreevna, Trofimov, Pishchik and Firs exit. Gaev, Varya and Yasha remain.

GAEV

My sister still has the habit of throwing money away. *(To Yasha)*
Back off, my dear fellow, you smell of chicken.

YASHA

(Laughs into his fist) And you, Leonid Andreich, are still the same
as ever.

GAEV

Whoso? *(To Varya)* What did he say?

VARYA

(To Yasha) Your mother has come from the village. She's been sitting
in the servants' quarters since yesterday, she wants to see you . . .

YASHA

As if I care!

VARYA

Shame on you!

YASHA

Who needs her. She could have come tomorrow. *(Exits)*

VARYA

Mama's still the same as ever, hasn't changed a bit. If she could,
she'd give everything away.

GAEV

Yes . . .

Pause.

If a great many remedies are prescribed against an illness, it means
the illness is incurable. I think, I wrack my brain, I have many remedies, a great many, which in fact means none. It would be nice to

27

get an inheritance from somebody, it would be nice to have our Anya marry a very rich man, it would be nice to go to Yaroslavl and try our luck with our aunt, the countess. The aunt's very, very rich.

VARYA

(Weeps) If only God would help us!

GAEV

Stop blubbering. The aunt's very rich, but she doesn't like us. First of all, my sister married a lawyer, not a nobleman . . .

Anya appears in the doorway.

Didn't marry a nobleman, and can't be said to have behaved herself all that virtuously. She's a kind woman, but, whatever extenuating circumstances you think up, still, you must admit she's depraved. You can sense it in her slightest movement.

VARYA

(Whispers) Anya's in the doorway.

GAEV

Whoso?

Pause.

Extraordinary, something's gotten into my right eye . . . I can't see very well. And on Thursday, when I was in the circuit court . . .

Anya enters.

VARYA

Why aren't you asleep, Anya?

ANYA

I don't feel like sleeping. I can't.

GAEV

My tiny one. *(Kisses Anya's face and hands)* My child . . . *(Through tears)* You're not my niece, you're my angel, you're everything to me. Believe me, believe me . . .

ANYA

I believe you, uncle. Everybody loves you, respects you . . . but, uncle dear, you must be quiet, just be quiet. What was it you said about my mother, about your sister? Why did you say that?

GAEV

Right, right . . . *(Covers his face with his hands)* It's really terrible! My God! God, save me! And the speech I made earlier to the bookcase . . . so stupid! And it was only when I finished that I realized it was stupid.

VARYA

It's true, uncle dear, you must be quiet. Just be quiet, that's all.

ANYA

If you're quiet, you'll feel calmer yourself.

GAEV

I'm quiet. *(Kisses Anya's and Varya's hands)* I'm quiet. There's just this one thing. On Thursday I was in the circuit court, well, so a group gathered, a conversation began about this and that, one thing led to another, and it seems it may be possible to arrange a loan on credit to pay off the interest to the bank.

VARYA

If only God would help us!

GAEV

I'll go on Tuesday and talk it over again. *(To Varya)* Stop blubbering. *(To Anya)* Your mother will talk to Lopakhin; he certainly won't refuse her . . . And you, once you've rested, will go to Yaroslavl, to the countess, your great-aunt. So we'll attack from three directions—and it's in the bag. We'll pay the interest, I'm sure of it . . . *(Puts a fruit drop in his mouth)* I swear on my honor, on anything you like, the estate will not be sold! I swear on my happiness. Here's my hand, call me a worthless, dishonorable man if I let it go up for auction! I swear on my whole being!

ANYA

You're so good, Uncle Lyonya, so intelligent! *(Embraces her uncle)* I'm at peace now! I'm at peace!

Firs enters.

FIRS

(Reproachfully) Leonid Andreich, have you no fear of God?! When are you going to bed?

GAEV

Right away, right away. You may go, Firs. Never mind, I'll undress myself. Well, children, bye-bye . . . Details tomorrow, but now go to bed. *(Kisses Anya and Varya)* I'm a man of the eighties . . . It's a time that's not much praised, but all I can say is, I've endured quite a lot for my convictions. It's not for nothing that the peasants love me. You've got to know the peasants! You've got to know how they . . .

ANYA

You're at it again, uncle!

VARYA

Quiet, uncle dear.

FIRS

(Crossly) Leonid Andreich!

GAEV

Coming, coming . . . Go to bed. Double bank shot into the side. Pot the clear ball . . . *(Exits. Firs trots along behind him)*

ANYA

I'm at peace now. I don't feel like going to Yaroslavl, I don't like my great-aunt, but all the same I'm at peace. Thanks to uncle. *(Sits down)*

VARYA

We must sleep. I'm going. There was some unpleasantness here while you were away. As you know, only the elderly servants live in the old servants' quarters: Efimyushka, Polya, Evstignei and Karp as well. They started letting some rascals spend the night with them—I said nothing. But then I hear they're spreading a rumor that I ordered them to be fed nothing but peas. Out of stinginess, you see . . . It's all Evstignei's doing . . . Very well, I think. In that case, I think, just you wait. I summon Evstignei . . . *(She yawns)* He comes . . . How is it, Evstignei, I say, fool that you are . . . *(Looks at Anya)* Anechka! . . .

Pause.

Asleep! . . . *(Takes Anya under the arm)* Let's go beddy-bye . . . Let's go! . . . *(Leads her)* My darling's asleep! Let's go! . . .

They start out. Far beyond the orchard, a shepherd is playing a pipe. Trofimov walks across the stage and, seeing Varya and Anya, stops.

VARYA

Shh . . . She's asleep . . . asleep . . . Let's go, my dearest.

ANYA

(Softly, half asleep) I'm so tired . . . these little bells . . . Uncle dear . . . and mama . . . and uncle . . .

VARYA

Let's go, my dearest, let's go . . . *(They exit to Anya's room)*

TROFIMOV

(Tenderly) My sunshine! My springtime!

Curtain.

ACT TWO

A field. An old, lopsided, long-abandoned chapel, next to it a well, big stones that apparently once used to be tombstones, and an old bench. You can see the road to Gaev's estate. To the side, some poplars hover darkly: the cherry orchard begins there. In the distance a row of telegraph poles, and far away on the horizon a big town is vaguely outlined, which can be seen only in very fine, clear weather. The sun will set soon. Yasha and Dunyasha sit on the bench. Epikhodov stands by them. Trofimov and Anya go past them on the way from the house.

ANYA

My great-aunt lives alone, she's very rich. She doesn't like mama. The first few days it was hard for me to be there, she barely spoke to me. But then she softened. Promised to send me money, gave me some for my and Charlotta's trip back. It's so eerie, so oppressive to feel you're a poor relation.

TROFIMOV

Looks like someone's here already . . . Sitting. In that case, let's go further on.

ANYA

I haven't been home for three weeks. How I missed it!

They exit.

EPIKHODOV

(Plays the guitar and sings) "What to me is the world and its noise, / what to me are friends and foes . . ." How nice to play the mandolin!

DUNYASHA

It's a guitar, not a mandolin.

EPIKHODOV

For a madman in love it's a mandolin . . . *(Sings under his breath)* "So long as my heart knows the joys / of ardent love in all its throes . . ."

Yasha sings along.

DUNYASHA

(To Yasha) Still, you're so lucky to have traveled abroad.

YASHA

Yes, of course. I cannot help but agree with you. *(Lights a cigar)*

EPIKHODOV

It's a known thing. Abroad everything has long since been in full completeness.

YASHA

That goes without saying.

Pause.

EPIKHODOV

I'm a cultivated man, I read all sorts of learned books, but I simply cannot understand where things are heading, and what in fact I want, to go on living or to shoot myself, but in any case, as a matter of fact, I always carry a revolver with me. Here it is . . . *(Shows the revolver)* As a matter of fact, regardless of other subjects, I must express about myself, by the way, that fate deals mercilessly with me, like a storm with a small boat. Supposing I'm mistaken, why then do I wake up this morning, for example, and see on my chest a spider of enormous proportions . . . This big. *(Shows with both hands)* Or I pick up a jug of kvass, so as to pour myself a drink, and there's something highly improper floating in it, like a cockroach.

Pause.

Have you read Buckle?

Pause.

I wish to trouble you, Avdotya Fyodorovna, with a couple of words.

DUNYASHA

Speak.

EPIKHODOV

It would be desirable for us to be alone . . . *(Sighs)*

DUNYASHA

(Embarrassed) Very well . . . only first bring me my little shawl . . . There by the cupboard . . . It's a bit damp here . . .

EPIKHODOV

Very well, miss . . . I'll bring it. Wonderful, miss . . . Now I know what to do with my revolver . . . *(Exits)*

YASHA

Two-and-twenty Catastrophes! A stupid man, just between us.

DUNYASHA

God forbid he shoots himself.

Pause.

I've become anxious, I worry all the time. I was still a little girl when I was taken into the masters' household, I'm unused to the simple life now, and look how white my hands are, like a young lady's. I've become so pampered, I'm afraid of everything . . . It's scary. And if you deceive me, Yasha, I don't know what will happen to me.

YASHA

(Kisses her) Cute little cucumber!

Pause.

Of course, every girl should remember herself, and what I dislike most of all is a girl who misbehaves. *(Hums a tune with no musical ear, then sings badly off key)* "Oh, wilt thou grasp the stirrings of my soul . . ."

DUNYASHA

I've fallen in love with you. You're cultivated. You can discuss everything.

Pause.

YASHA

(Yawns) Right, miss . . . My opinion is this: if a girl loves somebody, it means she's immoral. It's nice to smoke a cigar in the open air . . . *(Listens)* Somebody's coming . . . It's the masters . . . *(Hastily)* Come here tonight, when it's dark. Make sure you come . . .

Dunyasha embraces him impulsively.

Go home, as if you'd been swimming in the river, take this path, or else they'll see you and think we were here together. I couldn't stand that.

DUNYASHA

(Coughs softly) That cigar has given me a headache . . . *(Exits)*

Yasha stays, stands by the chapel. Lyubov Andreevna, Gaev and Lopakhin enter.

LOPAKHIN

You've got to decide once and for all—time is running out. The question is simple. Do you agree to lease the land for the construction of summer houses or do you not? Answer in one word: yes or no? Just one word!

LYUBOV ANDREEVNA

Who's been smoking disgusting cigars here . . . *(Sits down)*

GAEV

They've built the railroad, and it's become convenient. *(Sits down)* Rode into town and had lunch . . . yellow into the side! I'd like to go home first and play one game . . .

LYUBOV ANDREEVNA

There's no rush.

LOPAKHIN

Just one word! Give me an answer!

GAEV

(Yawning) Whoso?

LYUBOV ANDREEVNA

(Looking into her purse) Yesterday there was a lot of money, and today there's so little. My poor Varya saves money feeding everybody milk soup, in the kitchen the old folks get nothing but peas, and I waste money somehow senselessly . . . *(She drops her purse, gold coins spill out)* Go on, scatter . . . *(She is annoyed)*

YASHA

Allow me. I'll pick them up. *(Collects the coins)*

LYUBOV ANDREEVNA

Be so kind, Yasha. And why did I go to this lunch . . . Your trashy restaurant with its music, with its tablecloths stinking of soap . . . Why drink so much, Lyonya? Why eat so much? Why talk so much? Today in the restaurant you talked too much again, and all beside the point. About the seventies, about the decadents. And to whom? Talking to the waiters about the decadents!

LOPAKHIN

Hm, yes.

GAEV

(Waves his hand) I'm incorrigible, that's obvious . . . *(Vexedly, to Yasha)* Why are you constantly popping up in front of me . . .

YASHA

(Laughing into his fist) Just hearing your voice makes me laugh.

GAEV

(To his sister) It's either me, or him . . .

LYUBOV ANDREEVNA

Away with you, Yasha. Go, go . . .

YASHA

(Hands Lyubov Andreevna the purse) I'm leaving. *(Barely restraining his laughter)* Right now . . . *(Exits)*

LOPAKHIN

Rich man Deriganov intends to buy your estate. They say he'll come to the auction in person.

LYUBOV ANDREEVNA

Where did you hear that?

LOPAKHIN

There was talk in town.

GAEV

Our aunt in Yaroslavl has promised to send something, but when and how much nobody knows . . .

LOPAKHIN

How much will she send? A hundred thousand? Two hundred?

LYUBOV ANDREEVNA

Well . . . ten thousand—maybe fifteen, and be thankful for that.

LOPAKHIN

Forgive me, but I have never met such scatterbrained people, such strange, unbusinesslike people, as you two, my friends. I tell you in plain Russian that your estate is going to be sold, and it's as if you don't understand.

LYUBOV ANDREEVNA

What are we to do? Teach us what to do.

LOPAKHIN

I "teach" you every day. Every day I tell you one and the same thing. The cherry orchard and the land have got to be leased out for summer houses. It has got to be done now, as soon as possi-ble—the auction is almost upon us! Understand that! Once you finally decide to have summer houses, you'll get as much money as you like, and then you're saved.

LYUBOV ANDREEVNA

Summer houses, summer people—forgive me, but it's all so banal.

GAEV

I agree with you completely.

LOPAKHIN

I'm going to weep, or scream, or fall down in a faint! I can't stand it! You've worn me out! *(To Gaev)* You old woman!

GAEV

Whoso?

LOPAKHIN

Old woman! *(Starts to leave)*

LYUBOV ANDREEVNA

(Frightened) No, don't leave, stay with us, dear heart! I beg you. Maybe we'll think of something!

Varya and Charlotta Ivanovna pass by on the way from the house. Charlotta wears a man's visored cap and carries a gun.

VARYA

She's an intelligent and well-bred girl, nothing can happen, but still she should not be left alone with a young man. Supper's at nine o'clock, Charlotta Ivanovna, see that you're not late.

CHARLOTTA

I don't want to eat. *(Softly hums a song)*

VARYA

That doesn't matter. Just be there. Look, they're sitting there on the bank . . .

Varya and Charlotta exit.

LYUBOV ANDREEVNA

(To Lopakhin) Don't leave, dear heart. It's more cheerful with you here . . . I keep expecting something, as if the house is going to fall down on us.

GAEV

Double into the corner ... *Croisé* into the side ...

LYUBOV ANDREEVNA

We've sinned so very much ...

LOPAKHIN

What kind of sins do you have ...

GAEV

(Puts a fruit drop into his mouth) They say I ate up my whole fortune in fruit drops ... *(Laughs)*

LYUBOV ANDREEVNA

Oh, my sins ... I've always squandered money without stint, like a madwoman, and I married a man who did nothing but run up debts. My husband died from champagne—he drank terribly—and to my misfortune I fell in love with another man, took up with him, and just then—this was my first punishment, a blow right on the head—here, in this river ... my boy drowned, and I went abroad, for good, never to return, never to see this river ... I shut my eyes, I fled, forgetting myself, and *he* followed after me ... mercilessly, crudely. I bought a house near Menton, because he fell ill there, and for three years I got no rest day or night; the sick man wore me out, my soul dried up. And last year, once the cottage was sold for debts, I left for Paris, and there he fleeced me, abandoned me, took up with another woman, I tried to poison myself ... So stupid, so shameful ... And I suddenly felt drawn back to Russia, to my native land, to my little girl ... *(Wipes her tears)* Lord, Lord, have mercy, forgive me my sins! Don't punish me anymore! *(Takes a telegram from her pocket)* This came today from Paris ... He asks my forgiveness, begs me to come back. *(Tears up the telegram)* Sounds like music somewhere. *(Listens)*

GAEV

It's our famous Jewish band. Remember? Four fiddles, a flute and a double bass.

LYUBOV ANDREEVNA

It still exists? We should get them to come here sometime, arrange an evening.

LOPAKHIN

(Listens) I don't hear anything ... *(Hums softly)* "The Germans for some ready cash / will frenchify a Russky." *(Laughs)* What a play I saw last night in the theater—very funny.

LYUBOV ANDREEVNA

And most likely it wasn't funny at all. You shouldn't be looking at plays, you should take a look at yourselves. Your life is so gray, you say so much that's unnecessary.

LOPAKHIN

That's true. Let's come right out with it: our life is stupid ...

Pause.

My father was a peasant, an imbecile, he understood nothing, he taught me nothing, he just got drunk and beat me, and always with a stick. And essentially I'm the same sort of blockhead and imbecile. Never studied anything, my handwriting's vile, I'm ashamed to show people, like a pig's.

LYUBOV ANDREEVNA

You ought to get married, my friend.

LOPAKHIN

Yes ... That's true.

LYUBOV ANDREEVNA

Maybe to our Varya.

LOPAKHIN

Hm, yes.

LYUBOV ANDREEVNA

I took her from simple folk, she works all day, and the main thing is she loves you. And you've liked her since way back.

LOPAKHIN

Well, so? I'm willing . . .

Pause.

GAEV

I've been offered a post in the bank. Six thousand a year . . . Have you heard?

LYUBOV ANDREEVNA

Who, you? What an idea . . .

Firs enters bringing a coat.

FIRS

(To Gaev) Please put this on, sir, it's damp.

GAEV

(Puts on coat) I'm sick of you, brother.

FIRS

Ah, well . . . You left this morning without telling me. *(Looks him over)*

LYUBOV ANDREEVNA

How you've aged, Firs!

FIRS

If you please, ma'am.

LOPAKHIN

She says you've aged a lot!

43

FIRS

I've lived a long time. They were trying to get me married before your father came into the world . . . *(Laughs)* When we got our freedom, I was already head valet. I didn't accept freedom then, I stayed with my masters . . . I remember everybody was glad, but what they were glad about they didn't know themselves.

LOPAKHIN

It was very nice in the old days. At least they had flogging.

FIRS

(Not hearing well) Sure enough. Peasants with the masters, masters with the peasants, but now it's all gone to pieces, you can't figure anything out.

GAEV

Quiet, Firs. I have to go to town tomorrow. They've promised to introduce me to a certain general who can lend me money on credit.

LOPAKHIN

Nothing will come of it. And you won't pay the interest, don't worry.

LYUBOV ANDREEVNA

He's raving. There aren't any generals.

Trofimov, Anya and Varya enter.

GAEV

Look who's coming.

ANYA

Mama's sitting there.

LYUBOV ANDREEVNA

(Tenderly) Come here, come here . . . My darlings . . . *(Embraces Anya and Varya)* If you both only knew how I love you. Sit beside me. Here.

They all sit down.

LOPAKHIN

Our eternal student still goes around with young ladies.

TROFIMOV

That's none of your business.

LOPAKHIN

He'll be fifty soon, and he's still a student.

TROFIMOV

Quit your stupid jokes.

LOPAKHIN

Why're you getting angry, you odd duck?

TROFIMOV

Just stop badgering me.

LOPAKHIN

(Laughs) What do you think of me, if I may ask?

TROFIMOV

What I think is this, Ermolai Alexeich: you're a rich man, you'll soon be a millionaire. As there is a need in the food chain for predators who devour everything in their path, so there's a need for you.

Everybody laughs.

VARYA

Petya, why don't you tell us about planets.

LYUBOV ANDREEVNA

No, let's go on with yesterday's conversation.

TROFIMOV

About what?

GAEV

The proud man.

TROFIMOV

We talked for a long time yesterday, but we didn't come to any conclusion. According to you, there is something mystical about the proud man. Maybe, in your own way, you're right, but if we talk simply, without frills, what is there to be proud of? Does it even make sense when man's physiological constitution is none too good, when the vast majority of men are coarse, ignorant and profoundly unhappy? We must stop admiring ourselves. We must work.

GAEV

You die anyway.

TROFIMOV

Who knows? And what does it mean—to die? Maybe man has a hundred senses and death only kills off the five known to us, while the remaining ninety-five remain alive.

LYUBOV ANDREEVNA

You're so intelligent, Petya!

LOPAKHIN

(Ironically) Terribly!

TROFIMOV

The human race goes forward, perfecting its powers. One day all that's beyond its reach now will become close, clear, but we must work, we must give all our strength to helping those who seek the truth. Here in Russia very few are working right now. The vast majority of the intellectuals I know seek nothing, do nothing, and at the moment are unfit for work. They call themselves intellectuals, but they talk down to servants, treat peasants like animals, study poorly, read nothing serious, do precisely nothing, their science is only talk, and they have little understanding of art. They're all serious, they all have stern faces, they all talk only about important things, they philosophize, and meanwhile, in front of their eyes, workers eat disgusting food, sleep without pillows, thirty or forty to a room, with bedbugs everywhere, stench, dankness, moral filth . . . And all the nice talk is obviously aimed at distracting attention, our own and other people's. Show me where those day nurseries are that are talked about so much and so often? Where are the reading rooms? They're only written about in novels; in reality there aren't any. There's only dirt, banality, barbarism . . . Serious faces scare me; I don't like them. Serious conversations scare me. Better to be quiet.

LOPAKHIN

You know, I get up at five in the morning, work from morning till night, and I'm constantly dealing with money, my own and other people's, so I see what sort of people are around. You only need to start doing something, to realize how few honest, decent people there are. Sometimes, when I can't fall asleep, I think: "Lord, you gave us vast forests, boundless fields, the deepest horizons, and we who live here should be real giants ourselves . . ."

LYUBOV ANDREEVNA

What do you need giants for . . . They're only good in fairy tales, otherwise they're frightening.

Epikhodov passes by upstage.

(Pensively) There goes Epikhodov . . .

ANYA

(Pensively) There goes Epikhodov . . .

VARYA

Why is he living with us? He just keeps eating and drinks tea all day long.

LOPAKHIN

And makes plans to shoot himself.

LYUBOV ANDREEVNA

Well, I like Epikhodov. When he talks about his catastrophes, he makes me laugh. Don't dismiss him, Varya.

VARYA

It's impossible, mama! We have to dismiss the scoundrel.

GAEV

The sun has set, ladies and gentlemen.

TROFIMOV

Yes.

GAEV

(In a low voice, as if declaiming) O nature, wondrous nature, you shine with eternal radiance, beautiful and indifferent, you, whom we call mother, in yourself you combine being and death, you give life and you destroy . . .

VARYA

(Pleadingly) Uncle dear!

ANYA

You're at it again, uncle!

TROFIMOV

Better double the yellow into the side.

GAEV

I'll be quiet, I'll be quiet.

They all sit deep in thought. Silence. Only Firs's quiet muttering can be heard. Suddenly there is a distant sound, as if from the sky, the sound of a breaking string, dying away, sad.

LYUBOV ANDREEVNA

What was that?

LOPAKHIN

I don't know. Somewhere far away in a mine a bucket chain snapped. But somewhere very far away.

GAEV

Maybe it was some bird ... like a heron.

TROFIMOV

Or a barn owl ...

LYUBOV ANDREEVNA

(Shudders) It's unpleasant somehow.

Pause.

FIRS

It was the same before the catastrophe: the owl screeched, and the samovar went on whistling.

GAEV

Before what catastrophe?

FIRS

Freedom.

Pause.

LYUBOV ANDREEVNA

You know what, my friends, let's go, it's already evening. *(To Anya)* You have tears in your eyes ... What is it, my girl? *(Embraces her)*

ANYA

I just do, mama. It's nothing.

TROFIMOV

Somebody's coming.

A passerby appears in a shabby white cap and an overcoat, slightly drunk.

PASSERBY

May I ask if I can go straight to the station from here?

GAEV

You can. Just down this road.

PASSERBY

Much obliged to you. *(Coughs)* Splendid weather . . . *(Declaims)* Brother, my suffering brother . . . come down to the Volga, whose moaning . . . *(To Varya)* Mademoiselle, might a starving Russian have thirty kopecks . . .

Varya cries out in fear.

LOPAKHIN

(Angrily to himself) For every outrage, there's decency!

LYUBOV ANDREEVNA

(Nonplussed) Here . . . Take this . . . *(Rummages in her purse)* No silver . . . Never mind, here's a gold piece for you . . .

PASSERBY

Much obliged to you! *(Exits)*

Laughter.

VARYA

(Frightened) I'm leaving . . . I'm leaving . . . Oh, mama, the people at home have nothing to eat, and you gave him a gold piece.

LYUBOV ANDREEVNA

What can you do with a fool like me?! At home I'll give you all I have. Ermolai Alexeich, lend me some more! . . .

LOPAKHIN

Yes, ma'am.

LYUBOV ANDREEVNA

Let's go, ladies and gentlemen, it's time. And we've just made you a match here, Varya. Congratulations.

VARYA

(Through tears) You shouldn't joke about that, mama.

LOPAKHIN

Ofoolia, get thee to a nunnery . . .

GAEV

My hands are shaking: I haven't played billiards for so long.

LOPAKHIN

Ofoolia, O nymph, remember me in thy orisons!

LYUBOV ANDREEVNA

Let's go, ladies and gentlemen. It's nearly suppertime.

VARYA

He frightened me. My heart's pounding.

LOPAKHIN

I remind you, ladies and gentlemen: on August twenty-second the cherry orchard will go up for sale. Think about it! . . . Think! . . .

Exit all but Trofimov and Anya.

ANYA

(Laughing) Thanks to that man who frightened Varya, we're alone now.

TROFIMOV

Varya's afraid we'll up and fall in love with each other. With her narrow mind, she can't understand that we're higher than love. To go beyond the petty and illusory that keep us from being free and happy—that is the goal and meaning of our life. Forward! We go irrepressibly towards the bright star that shines there in the distance! Forward! Don't lag behind, my friends!

ANYA

(Clasping her hands) How well you speak!

Pause.

It's wonderful here today!

TROFIMOV

Yes, the weather is astonishing.

ANYA

What have you done to me, Petya? Why don't I love the cherry orchard the way I used to? I loved it so dearly, I thought there was no better place on earth than our orchard.

TROFIMOV

All Russia is our orchard. The earth is vast and beautiful, there are many marvelous places on it.

Pause.

Think, Anya: your grandfather, your great-grandfather, and all your ancestors were serf-owners, owners of human souls. Can it be that human beings don't look at you from every cherry, from every leaf, from every tree trunk of this orchard, that you don't hear their voices? . . . To own living souls—it transformed you all, those who lived before and those living now, so that your mother, you, your uncle no longer notice that you are living on credit, at the expense of others, at the expense of people you won't allow across your threshold . . . We're at least two hundred years behind, we still have precisely nothing, no definite attitude towards the past. We only philosophize, complain of our anguish, or drink vodka. Yet it's so clear that to begin to live in the present, we must first atone for our past, be done with it, and we can only atone for it through suffering, only through extraordinary, relentless labor. Understand that, Anya.

ANYA

For a long time now the house we live in hasn't been ours, and I shall leave, I give you my word.

TROFIMOV

If you have the keys of the household, throw them down the well and walk away. Be free as the wind.

ANYA

(Ecstatically) How well you put it!

TROFIMOV

Shh. Somebody's coming. That Varya again! *(Angrily)* Outrageous!

ANYA

Well, then . . . Let's go to the river. It's nice there.

TROFIMOV

Let's go.

ANYA

(As they go) The moon will rise soon. *(They exit)*

Firs enters, then Charlotta Ivanovna. Firs, muttering, is looking for something on the ground by the bench, lights a match.

FIRS

(Mutters) Eh, you . . . blunderhead.

CHARLOTTA

(Sits down on the bench and takes off her cap) Is that you, Firs? What are you looking for?

FIRS

Mistress lost her purse.

CHARLOTTA

(Looking) Here's a fan ... and a handkerchief ... smells of perfume.

Pause.

There's nothing else. Lyubov Andreevna constantly loses things. She's lost her life, too. *(Softly hums a song)* I don't have a real passport, grandpa, I don't know how old I am, and I keep imaging I'm a young girl ... *(Puts the cap on Firs's head; he doesn't move)* Oh how I love you, my dear mister! *(Laughs) Eins, zwei, drei! (Takes the cap off Firs's head, puts it on her own)* When I was little, my father and mother went around to fairs and gave performances, very good ones. And I did the *salto mortale* and various things like that. And when father and mother died, a German lady took me in and began to teach me. Right. I grew up, then I went to be a governess. But where I'm from and who I am—I don't know ... Who my parents were, and whether they were even married ... I don't know ... *(Takes a cucumber out of her pocket and eats)* I don't know anything.

FIRS

I was twenty or twenty-five, and so we walked there, me, and the deacon's son, and the cook Vassily, and there was a man sitting on a stone ... an unknown man, a stranger ... I got scared for some reason and left, and then they up and killed him ... He had money.

CHARLOTTA

So? *Weiter.*

FIRS

Then there was a trial, interrogations . . . They arrested them . . .
And me, too . . . I was in prison for about two years . . . Then it was
all right, they let me out . . . That was long ago.

Pause.

A man can't remember everything . . .

CHARLOTTA

It's time for you to die, grandpa. *(Eats the cucumber)*

FIRS

Eh? *(Mutters to himself)* Well, so we went there all together, then
had to stop . . . Uncle jumped off the cart . . . took a sack . . . and
inside there was another sack. He looked in, and something inside
went—wiggle-wiggle!

CHARLOTTA

(Laughs softly) Wiggle-wiggle! *(Eats the cucumber)*

*There is a sound of someone walking down the road and softly play-
ing the balalaika . . . The moon is rising. Somewhere by the poplars
Varya is looking for Anya and calling: "Anya! Where are you?"*
    Curtain.

ACT THREE

The drawing room, separated by an archway from the ballroom. The chandelier is lit. A Jewish band, the same one mentioned in the second act, is playing in the front hall.

Evening. People in the ballroom are dancing a grand-rond. The voice of Simeonov-Pishchik: "Promenade à une paire!" Dancing couples come out into the drawing room: first Pishchik and Charlotta, then Trofimov and Lyubov Andreevna, then Anya and the postal clerk, then Varya and the stationmaster, and so on. Varya quietly weeps and wipes her tears as she dances. Dunyasha is in the last couple. They go back into the ballroom. Pishchik calls out: "Grand-rond, balancez!" and "Les cavaliers à genoux et remerciez vos dames!"

Firs, dressed in a tailcoat, serves seltzer water on a tray. Pishchik and Trofimov enter the drawing room.

PISHCHIK

My heart's pumping, I've already had two strokes, it's hard for me to dance, but, as they say, when you run with the pack, there's no

57

turning back. Still, I'm healthy as a horse. My late father, may he rest in peace, liked to joke. He used to say that our ancient family of the Simeonov-Pishchiks goes back to that very same horse Caligula gave a seat to in the Senate . . . *(Sits down)* But the trouble is: no money! A hungry dog believes only in meat . . . *(Snores and wakes up at once)* Same with me . . . only it's money . . .

TROFIMOV

In fact, you do have a certain horsey look.

PISHCHIK

Well, so . . . the horse is a good beast . . . you can sell a horse . . .

The sound of billiards comes from the next room. Varya appears under the archway of the ballroom.

TROFIMOV

(Teasing) Madame Lopakhin! Madame Lopakhin! . . .

VARYA

(Angrily) Mangy mister!

TROFIMOV

Yes, I'm a mangy mister, and proud of it!

VARYA

(Pondering bitterly) We've hired musicians, and how are we going to pay them? *(Exits)*

TROFIMOV

(To Pishchik) If you had found some other use for all the energy you've spent in the course of your life scraping up the money to pay your interest, you might have stood the world on its head.

PISHCHIK

Nietzsche . . . a philosopher . . . the greatest, the most famous . . . a man of vast intelligence, says in his writings that it's permitted to make counterfeit money.

TROFIMOV

So you've read Nietzsche?

PISHCHIK

Well . . . Dashenka told me. And I'm in such a position now that I might as well go and start counterfeiting . . . In two days I have to pay back three hundred and ten roubles . . . I've already got hold of a hundred and thirty . . . *(Feels anxiously in his pockets)* The money's vanished! I've lost the money! *(Through tears)* Where's the money? *(Joyfully)* Ah, here it is, in the lining . . . I even broke into a sweat . . .

Lyubov Andreevna and Charlotta Ivanovna enter.

LYUBOV ANDREEVNA

(Humming a lively Georgian dance tune) Why is Leonid taking so long? What's he doing in town? *(To Dunyasha)* Dunyasha, offer the musicians some tea . . .

TROFIMOV

The auction probably didn't take place.

LYUBOV ANDREEVNA

It was the wrong time for musicians, the wrong time for a ball . . . Well, never mind . . . *(Sits down and hums softly)*

CHARLOTTA

(Hands Pishchik a deck of cards) Here's a deck of cards, think of a card, any card.

PISHCHIK

Ready.

CHARLOTTA

Now shuffle the deck. Very good. Now give it to me, my dear Mr. Pishchik. *Eins, zwei, drei!* Now look in your side pocket, it's there . . .

PISHCHIK

(Takes a card from his side pocket) The eight of spades, absolutely right! *(Surprised)* Imagine that!

CHARLOTTA

(Holds the deck out on her palm to Trofimov) Tell me quickly, which card is on top?

TROFIMOV

Oh, let's say the queen of spades.

CHARLOTTA

Right! *(Shows the queen of spades; to Lyubov Andreevna)* Tell me quickly! Quickly!

LYUBOV ANDREEVNA

The ten of diamonds.

CHARLOTTA

Right! *(Shows the ten of diamonds)* Eins, zwei, drei! *(Slaps her palm, the deck of cards disappears)* What nice weather today!

A mysterious woman's voice answers her as if from underground: "Oh, yes, magnificent weather, my lady."

You're so nice, my ideal man . . .

The voice: "I am also liking you very much, my lady."

How do you do?

"Oh, when I saw you, my heart began to ache very much!"

LYUBOV ANDREEVNA

(Applauds) Bravo, bravo!

The whole room applauds.

PISHCHIK

(Surprised) Imagine that! Most charming Charlotta Ivanovna . . . I'm simply in love with you . . .

CHARLOTTA

In love? *(Shrugging)* So you're able to love? *Guter Mensch, aber schlechter Musikant.*

PISHCHIK

Well, I don't understand your *schlechter-mechter.* Today Lyubov Andreevna will kindly lend me a hundred and eighty roubles . . . That I understand . . .

LYUBOV ANDREEVNA

As if I have any money! Leave me alone.

TROFIMOV

(Slaps Pishchik on the shoulder) There's a good horse . . .

CHARLOTTA

Attention please, one more trick. *(Takes a blanket from a chair)* Here's a very fine blanket. Not a hole in it, not a spot. A very fine blanket. I have the wish to sell it . . . *(Holds it up)* Does anyone wish to buy it?

PISHCHIK

(Surprised) Imagine that!

CHARLOTTA

Eins, zwei, drei!

She quickly moves the blanket aside; behind it stands Anya. She curtsies, runs to her mother, embraces her, and runs back to the ballroom amidst general delight.

LYUBOV ANDREEVNA

(Applauds) Bravo, bravo! . . .

CHARLOTTA

Once more now! *Eins, zwei, drei!*

She moves the blanket aside; Varya is standing behind it and bows.

PISHCHIK

(Surprised) Imagine that!

CHARLOTTA

The end! *(Throws the blanket over Pishchik, curtseys, and runs off to the ballroom)*

PISHCHIK

(Hurries after her) Wicked woman . . . isn't she? Isn't she? *(Exits)*

LYUBOV ANDREEVNA

And still no Leonid. What he's doing so long in town, I don't understand. Everything must be finished there, the estate has been sold, or the auction didn't take place. Why keep me in the dark for so long?!

VARYA

Uncle has bought it, I'm sure of that.

TROFIMOV

(Mockingly) Oh, yes.

VARYA

Our great-aunt sent him the power of attorney to buy it in her name with the transfer of the debt. She did it for Anya. And I'm sure, with God's help, uncle will buy it.

LYUBOV ANDREEVNA

Your great-aunt from Yaroslavl! She sent fifteen thousand to buy the estate in *her* name—she doesn't trust us—and that money isn't even enough to pay the interest. *(Covers her face with her hands)* Today my fate is being decided, my fate . . .

TROFIMOV

(Teases Varya) Madame Lopakhin!

VARYA

(Angrily) Eternal student! Already expelled twice from the university.

LYUBOV ANDREEVNA

Why do you get angry, Varya? He teases you about Lopakhin—what of it? Marry Lopakhin, if you want to. He's a good, interesting man. If you don't want to—don't. Nobody's forcing you, my sweet . . .

VARYA

For me it's a very serious matter, mama, to be honest. He's a good man, I like him.

LYUBOV ANDREEVNA

So marry him. I don't understand what you're waiting for!

VARYA

But, mama, I can't propose to him myself. For two years now everybody's been talking to me about him. Everybody talks, but he either says nothing or makes jokes. I understand. He's getting rich, he's busy, he can't be bothered with me. If only I had some money, just a little, just a hundred roubles, I'd drop everything, I'd go far, far away. I'd go to a convent.

TROFIMOV

What blessedness!

VARYA

(To Trofimov) Students are supposed to be intelligent! *(In a soft voice, through tears)* How unattractive you've become, Petya, how you've aged! *(To Lyubov Andreevna, no longer tearful)* Only I can't just sit idle, mama. I have to be doing something every minute.

Yasha enters.

YASHA

(Barely able to keep from laughing) Epikhodov just broke a billiard cue! . . . *(Exits)*

VARYA

What is Epikhodov doing here? Who allowed him to play billiards? I don't understand these people . . . *(Exits)*

LYUBOV ANDREEVNA

Don't tease her, Petya. You can see she's unhappy as it is.

TROFIMOV

She's so officious, always poking her nose into other people's business. She hasn't left Anya and me alone all summer, for fear we might start a romance. What business is it of hers? Besides, I never gave any sign of it, I'm far from such banality. We're higher than love!

LYUBOV ANDREEVNA

Then I must be lower than love. *(In great anxiety)* Why isn't Leonid here? If only I knew whether the estate's been sold or not! This catastrophe seems so incredible to me, I somehow don't even know what to think, I'm at a loss . . . I could scream . . . I could do something stupid. Save me, Petya. Say something, go on, say something . . .

TROFIMOV

Does it make any difference whether the estate gets sold today or not? It was all finished long ago, there's no turning back, the path is overgrown. Calm down, my dear. Don't deceive yourself. You must face the truth at least once in your life.

LYUBOV ANDREEVNA

What truth? You can see where truth is and where it isn't. You boldly resolve all the important questions, but isn't that because you're young, because you haven't had time to suffer for a single one of your questions? You boldly look ahead, but isn't that because you don't see or expect anything terrible, because you still don't know life? You're bolder, more honest, more generous than we are, but let's leave that . . . Think about it, show just a tiny bit of generosity, have mercy on me. I was born here, my father and mother lived here, and my grandfather, I love this house, I can't conceive of my life without the cherry orchard, and if it's so necessary to sell it, then sell me along with it . . . *(Embraces Trofimov, kisses him on the forehead)* My son drowned here . . . *(Weeps)* You're a good, kind man: have pity on me.

TROFIMOV

You know I sympathize with all my heart.

LYUBOV ANDREEVNA

Yes, but couldn't you . . . couldn't you say it some other way? . . . *(Takes out a handkerchief, a telegram falls on the floor)* My soul is weighed down today, you can't imagine. It's noisy for me here, my soul trembles at every sound, I tremble all over, but I can't go to my room, I'm afraid to be alone in the silence. Don't judge me, Petya . . . I love you like one of my own. I'd gladly have you marry Anya, I swear I would, only you must study, darling, you must finish your education. You don't do anything, it's so strange . . . Isn't it? And you should do something about your beard, make it grow somehow . . . *(Laughs)* You're so funny!

TROFIMOV

(Picks up the telegram) I have no wish to be handsome.

LYUBOV ANDREEVNA

It's a telegram from Paris. I get one every day. One yesterday, one today. This savage man is sick again, things are going badly again . . . He asks my forgiveness, begs me to come back, and I really ought to go to Paris and be with him. You're making a stern face, Petya, but what am I to do, darling, what am I to do, he's ill, he's lonely, unhappy, and who will look after him, who will keep him from making mistakes, who will give him his medicine on time? And why hide it or keep silent? I love him, it's obvious. I love him, I love him ... He's a millstone around my neck, he's dragging me down with him, but I love this stone and can't live without it. *(She presses Trofimov's hand)* Don't think ill of me, Petya, don't say anything to me, don't ...

TROFIMOV

(Through tears) Forgive my frankness, but, for God's sake, the man fleeced you!

LYUBOV ANDREEVNA

No, no, no, you mustn't speak that way ... *(Covers her ears)*

TROFIMOV

He's a scoundrel, you're the only one who doesn't know it! He's a petty scoundrel, a nothing ...

LYUBOV ANDREEVNA

(Angrily, but restraining herself) You're twenty-six or twenty-seven years old, but you're still a schoolboy!

TROFIMOV

So what if I am!

LYUBOV ANDREEVNA

You should be a man, at your age you should understand what it is to love. And you yourself should love ... you should fall in love! *(Angrily)* Yes, yes! You're not all that pure, you're just a squeamish, silly, eccentric little freak ...

TROFIMOV

(Horrified) What is she saying!

LYUBOV ANDREEVNA

"I'm higher than love!" You're not higher than love, you're simply, as our Firs here says, a blunderhead. Not to have a mistress at your age! ...

TROFIMOV

(Horrified) This is terrible! What is she saying?! *(Goes quickly toward the ballroom, clutching his head)* This is terrible . . . I can't stand it, I'm leaving . . . It's all over between us! *(Exits to the front hall)*

LYUBOV ANDREEVNA

(Shouts after him) Petya, wait! Silly man, I was joking! Petya!

The sound of someone's quick steps on the stairs, then a sudden crash. Anya and Varya cry out, but at once laughter is heard.

What was that?

Anya runs in.

ANYA

(Laughing) Petya fell down the stairs! *(Runs out)*

LYUBOV ANDREEVNA

What a funny one this Petya is . . . *(Follows her out)*

The stationmaster stands in the middle of the ballroom and recites "The Sinful Woman," by A. K. Tolstoy:

STATIONMASTER

Mirth and laughter from the crowd,
Lutes and cymbals ringing loud,
Flowers and garlands all around,
Brocade curtains hanging down,
Brightly trimmed with gleaming braid,
Palace halls richly arrayed,
Gold and crystal everywhere . . .

They all listen, but after he has read a few lines, the sounds of a waltz come from the front hall and the reading breaks off. They all dance. Trofimov, Anya, Varya and Lyubov Andreevna come from the front hall.

LYUBOV ANDREEVNA

Well, Petya . . . you pure soul . . . I ask your forgiveness . . . Let's dance . . . *(Dances with Petya)*

Anya and Varya dance. Firs enters, places his stick by the side door. Yasha also enters and watches the dancing.

YASHA

What is it, grandpa?

FIRS

Not feeling well. In the old days we had generals and admirals dancing at our balls, and now we send for the postal clerk and the stationmaster, and even they aren't so eager to come. I've grown a bit weak. My late master, the grandfather, treated everybody with sealing wax, for all ailments. I've been taking sealing wax every day for twenty years, if not more; maybe that's why I'm still alive.

YASHA

I'm sick of you, grandpa. *(Yawns)* Why don't you just up and croak . . .

FIRS

Eh, you . . . blunderhead! *(Mutters)*

Trofimov and Lyubov Andreevna dance in the ballroom, then in the drawing room.

LYUBOV ANDREEVNA

Merci. I'll sit for a while . . . *(Sits down)* I'm tired.

Anya enters.

ANYA

A man in the kitchen said just now that the cherry orchard was sold today.

LYUBOV ANDREEVNA

Sold to whom?

ANYA

He didn't say. He left. *(Dances with Trofimov, both exit to the ball-room)*

YASHA

It was some old man there babbling. A stranger.

FIRS

And Leonid Andreich still isn't here, he hasn't come. He's wearing a light coat, demi-season, he's likely to catch cold. Ehh, green youth!

LYUBOV ANDREEVNA

I'm going to die right here and now. Go, Yasha, find out who bought it.

YASHA

But the old man's long gone. *(Laughs into his fist)*

LYUBOV ANDREEVNA

(Slightly annoyed) Well, what are you laughing at? What are you glad about?

YASHA

Epikhodov's so funny. Two-and-twenty Catastrophes.

LYUBOV ANDREEVNA

If the estate is sold, Firs, where will you go?

FIRS

Wherever you tell me.

LYUBOV ANDREEVNA

Why such a face? Are you unwell? You know, you should go to bed . . .

FIRS

Oh, yes ... *(With a grin)* I'll go to bed, and who will serve here without me, who'll be in charge? I'm the only one in the whole house.

YASHA

(To Lyubov Andreevna) Lyubov Andreevna! Please allow me to address you with a request. If you go back to Paris, do me the favor of taking me with you. It is absolutely impossible for me to remain here. *(Looking around, in a low voice)* Judge for yourself, it's an uneducated country, the people are immoral, and besides it's boring, they feed us execrably in the kitchen, and then there's this Firs going around muttering all sorts of inanities. Please take me with you!

Pishchik enters.

PISHCHIK

Allow me to invite you ... for a little waltz, most excellent lady ... *(Lyubov Andreevna gets up and dances with him)* Charming lady, I'll still get a hundred and eighty little roubles from you ... I will ... *(Dances)* A hundred and eighty little roubles ...

They pass into the ballroom.

YASHA

(Humming softly) "Oh, wilt thou grasp the stirrings of my soul ..."

In the ballroom, a figure in a gray top hat, a tail coat and checkered trousers leaps and waves its arms; there are shouts of: "Bravo, Charlotta Ivanovna!"

DUNYASHA

(Stops to powder her nose; tries to do it discreetly) The young miss told me to dance—there are lots of gentlemen, and not enough ladies—and I get dizzy from dancing, my heart is pounding, Firs Nikolaevich, and the postal clerk just said something to me that took my breath away.

The music dies down.

FIRS

What did he say to you?

DUNYASHA

You, he said, are like a flower.

YASHA

(Laughs into his fist) Ignorance ... *(Exits)*

DUNYASHA

Like a flower ... *(Through tears)* I'm terribly fond of tender words.

FIRS

You'll take a tumble.

Epikhodov enters.

EPIKHODOV

So you don't want to see me, Avdotya Fyodorovna ... as if I'm some sort of insect. *(Sighs)* Life!

DUNYASHA

What can I do for you?

EPIKHODOV

Doubtless, you may be right. *(Sighs)* But if you look at it from the point of view, then, if I may put it so, forgive my frankness, you absolutely drove me into a state of mind. I know my fortune, every day some sort of catastrophe befalls me, and to that I have long been accustomed, so that I look upon my fate with a smile. You gave me your word, and though, nevertheless, I ...

DUNYASHA

Let's talk someplace else, I beg you ...

EPIKHODOV

Catastrophes happen to me every day, and, if I may put it so, I only smile, even laugh, but . . .

Varya enters from the ballroom.

VARYA

You still haven't left, Semyon? Really, how can you be so disrespectful! *(To Dunyasha)* Go, Dunyasha. *(To Epikhodov)* First you play billiards and break a cue, then you strut around the drawing room as if you're a guest.

EPIKHODOV

You can't exact anything from me, if I may put it so.

VARYA

I'm not "exacting" anything from you, I'm telling you. All you do is wander around from place to place, and you don't do any work. We keep a clerk, but who knows why.

EPIKHODOV

(Offended) Whether I work, or wander, or eat, or play billiards— that can be discussed only by mature and understanding people.

VARYA

How dare you say that to me! *(Flaring up)* How dare you! So I don't understand anything? Get out of here! This minute!

EPIKHODOV

(Turning coward) I ask you to express yourself in a more delicate manner.

VARYA

(Beside herself) Get out of here, this very minute! Out, scoundrel!

He goes toward the door; she follows him.

Two-and-twenty Catastrophes! Don't you set foot in here again. Don't let me lay eyes on you!

Epikhodov exits; his voice comes from outside the door: "I shall lodge a complaint against you."

Ah, so you're coming back? *(Grabs the stick Firs has left by the door)* Come on, then . . . come on . . . come on, I'll show you . . . Ah, so you're coming? You're really coming? Take this then . . . *(She swings the stick. The blow lands on Lopakhin, who enters just then)*

LOPAKHIN

My humble thanks.

VARYA

(Angrily and mockingly) Very sorry!

LOPAKHIN

Never mind, miss. I humbly thank you for the pleasant treatment.

VARYA

Don't mention it. *(Steps away, then looks at him and asks softly)* Did I hurt you badly?

LOPAKHIN

No, it's nothing. It'll give me a hu-u-uge bump, though.

Voices in the ballroom: "Lopakhin's here! Ermolai Alexeich!"

PISHCHIK

Ah, long have we waited, long have we wondered . . . *(Exchanges kisses with Lopakhin)* There's a whiff of cognac coming off you, my dear heart. We're having a good time here, too.

Lyubov Andreevna enters.

LYUBOV ANDREEVNA

It's you, Ermolai Alexeich? What took you so long? Where's Leonid?

LOPAKHIN

Leonid Andreich arrived with me, he's coming . . .

LYUBOV ANDREEVNA

(Nervously) Well, so? Did the auction take place? Tell me!

LOPAKHIN

(Embarrassed, afraid of displaying his joy) The auction was over by four o'clock . . . We missed the train, had to wait for the nine-thirty. *(With a heavy sigh)* Oof! I'm still a bit giddy . . . We drank cognac.

Gaev enters; he is holding his purchases in his right hand and wiping his tears with his left.

LYUBOV ANDREEVNA

Lyonya, what is it? Well, Lyonya? *(Impatiently, with tears)* Quickly, for God's sake . . .

GAEV

(Makes no reply, only waves his hand; to Firs, weeping) Here, take them . . . There are anchovies, Kerch herring . . . I haven't eaten at all today . . . What I've been through!

The door to the billiard room is open; the click of billiard balls is heard and Yasha's shout: "Seven and eighteen!" Gaev's expression changes; he no longer weeps.

I'm awfully tired. Bring me a change of clothes, Firs. *(Goes through the ballroom to his own room. Firs follows)*

PISHCHIK

What happened at the auction? Tell us!

LYUBOV ANDREEVNA

Was the cherry orchard sold?

LOPAKHIN

Yes, it was.

LYUBOV ANDREEVNA

Who bought it?

LOPAKHIN

I bought it.

Pause.

Lyubov Andreevna is crushed; she would have fallen if she had not been standing by an armchair and a table. Varya takes the keys from her belt, flings them onto the floor in the middle of the drawing room, and exits.

I bought it! Wait, ladies and gentlemen, please, my head's in a fog, I can't speak . . . *(Laughs)* We came to the auction, Deriganov was already there. Leonid Andreich only had fifteen thousand, and Deriganov immediately bid thirty on top of the debt. I see how it goes, I take him up on it and bid forty. He goes up to forty-five. I go up to fifty-five. He keeps adding five, I keep adding ten . . . Well, in the end I bid ninety on top of the debt, and I got it. The cherry orchard's mine now! Mine! *(Laughs loudly)* Oh, Lord God, the cherry orchard's mine! Tell me I'm drunk, I'm out of my mind, I'm imagining it all . . . *(Stamps his feet)* Don't laugh at me! No, no, don't! If only my father and grandfather could rise from their graves and look at this whole thing, at their Ermolai, their beaten, barely literate Ermolai, who ran around barefoot in the winter, at how this same Ermolai bought the estate, than which there's nothing more beautiful in the world. I bought the estate where my grandfather and father were slaves, where they weren't even allowed into the kitchen. I'm dreaming, I'm making it up, it only seems so . . . It's the fruit of your imagination, covered in the darkness of the unknown . . . *(Picks up the keys)* She threw down the keys. She wants to show she's no longer in charge here . . . *(Jingles the keys)* Well, it makes no difference. Hey, musicians, play, let's hear it! Come on, everybody, watch Ermolai Lopakhin take the axe to the cherry orchard, watch the trees fall down! We'll build summer houses, and our grandchildren and great-grandchildren will see a new life here . . . Music, play!

Music plays. Lyubov Andreevna sinks into a chair and weeps bitterly.

(To her, with reproach) Why, why didn't you listen to me? My poor dear, there's no going back now. *(In tears)* Oh, if only all this could be over quickly, if only our senseless, luckless life could change quickly.

PISHCHIK
(Takes him under the arm, in a half whisper) She's crying. Let's go to the ballroom and leave her alone . . . Come on. *(Takes him under the arm and leads him to the ballroom)*

LOPAKHIN
What's going on? Music, louder! Let everything be the way I want it! *(With irony)* Here comes the new landlord, the owner of the cherry orchard! *(Accidentally shoves a little table, almost tips over the candelabra)* I can pay for everything! *(Exits with Pishchik)*

There is no one in the ballroom and the drawing room except Lyubov Andreevna, who sits huddled up and weeps bitterly. Music plays softly. Anya and Trofimov enter quickly. Anya goes to her mother and kneels before her. Trofimov remains by the entrance to the ballroom.

ANYA
Mama! . . . Mama, you're crying? My dear, kind, good mama, my beautiful mama, I love you . . . I bless you. The cherry orchard's been sold, it's no more, that's true, that's true, but don't cry, mama,

you still have your life ahead of you, you still have your good, pure soul . . . Come with me, come, dearest, let's go away from here, come! . . . We'll plant a new orchard, more luxuriant than this one, you'll see it, you'll understand, and joy, a quiet, deep joy, will descend into your soul, like the sun at evening, and you'll smile, mama! Come, my dear! Come! . . .

Curtain.

ACT FOUR

———

Large room on the ground floor. There is no chandelier, there are no paintings on the walls; there is some furniture left, piled up in one corner as if for a sale. There is a feeling of emptiness. Suitcases, bundles, and so on are piled up by the exit door and at the back of the stage. The door to the left is open; Varya and Anya's voices come from there. Lopakhin stands waiting. Yasha holds a tray of glasses filled with champagne. In the front hall Epikhodov is tying up a box. Noise comes from deep backstage. It is peasants who have come to say good-bye. Gaev's voice says: "Thank you, brothers, thank you."

YASHA
The simple folk have come to say good-bye. My opinion is this, Ermolai Alexeich: they're good folk, but they understand very little.

The noise dies down. Lyubov Andreevna and Gaev enter through the front hall. She no longer weeps, but she is pale, her face twitches, and she is unable to speak.

GAEV

You gave them your purse, Lyuba. Impossible! Impossible!

LYUBOV ANDREEVNA

I couldn't help it! I couldn't help it!

Both exit.

LOPAKHIN

(Through the doorway, calls after them) Wait, I humbly beg you! A little glass for the road. I didn't think to bring it from town, and they only had one bottle at the station. Wait!

Pause.

So, you don't want to? *(Steps away from the door)* If I'd known, I wouldn't have bought it. Well, I won't drink either, then.

Yasha carefully sets the tray on a chair.

Yasha, you drink at least.

YASHA

To those who are leaving! Good luck to those who are staying! *(He drinks)* This is not real champagne, I can assure you.

LOPAKHIN

Eight roubles a bottle.

Pause.

It's damned cold here.

YASHA

Didn't heat it today. We're leaving anyway. *(Laughs into his fist)*

LOPAKHIN

What's with you?

YASHA

I'm delighted.

LOPAKHIN

It's October, but sunny and calm, like summer. Good for building. *(Glancing at his watch, says through the door)* Bear in mind, ladies and gentlemen, that the train comes in forty-six minutes! Which means you should leave for the station in twenty minutes. Hurry it up.

Trofimov enters from outside wearing an overcoat.

TROFIMOV

I suppose it's already time to go. They've brought the horses. Devil knows where my galoshes are. Vanished. *(Through the door)* Anya, where are my galoshes? I can't find them!

LOPAKHIN

And I must go to Kharkov. I'm taking the same train as you. I'll spend the whole winter in Kharkov. All this hanging around with you and doing nothing has worn me out. I can't get by without work, I don't know what to do with my hands, they hang there somehow strangely, like somebody else's.

TROFIMOV

We'll be gone soon, and you can go back to your useful labors.

LOPAKHIN

Have a little glass.

TROFIMOV

None for me.

LOPAKHIN

So, it's Moscow now?

TROFIMOV

Yes, I'll see them off in town, and tomorrow it's Moscow.

LOPAKHIN

Yes . . . No doubt the professors are holding off their lectures, waiting for you to come!

TROFIMOV

That's none of your business.

LOPAKHIN

How many years have you been studying at the university?

TROFIMOV

Try thinking up something new. That's old and stale. *(Pause)* You know, we may just never see each other again, so allow me to give you a piece of parting advice: stop waving your arms! Get out of this habit of waving your arms. And building summer houses, calculating that in time the summer people will turn into independent farmers, calculating like that—is also waving your arms . . . Anyhow, I still like you. You have fine, delicate fingers, like an artist; you have a fine, delicate soul . . .

LOPAKHIN

(Embraces him) Good-bye, dear boy. Thanks for everything. Take some money from me for the road, if you need it.

TROFIMOV

Why should I? There's no need.

LOPAKHIN

But you haven't got any!

TROFIMOV

Yes, I have. Thanks very much. I got some for a translation. It's right here in my pocket. *(Anxiously)* But where are my galoshes?!

VARYA

(From the other room) Here, take the vile things! *(Throws a pair of rubber galoshes onto the stage)*

TROFIMOV

What are you angry about, Varya? Hm . . . No, these aren't my galoshes.

LOPAKHIN

I sowed three thousand acres of poppies in the spring, and just made forty thousand. When my poppies flowered, what a picture it was! So, as I say, I made forty thousand, and I'm offering to lend you some, because I can. Why turn up your nose? I'm a peasant . . . let's keep it simple.

TROFIMOV

Your father was a peasant, mine was a druggist, and from that follows—absolutely nothing.

Lopakhin takes out his wallet.

Stop, stop . . . I won't take it, even if it's two hundred thousand. I'm a free man. Nothing that all of you, rich and poor, value so highly and dearly, has the least power over me, any more than this bit of fluff floating in the air. I can get along without you, I can pass you by, I'm strong and proud. Mankind is striding towards the highest truth, towards the highest happiness possible on earth, and I am in the forefront!

LOPAKHIN

Will you get there?

TROFIMOV

I will get there, or I will show others the way.

The sound of an axe striking wood is heard.

LOPAKHIN

Well, good-bye, dear boy. It's time to go. Here we are turning up our noses at each other, and meanwhile life is passing by. When I work for a long time without a break, my thoughts become lighter, and it seems as if I also know why I exist. But there are so many people in Russia, brother, who exist with no idea why. Well, never mind, that's not what keeps things circulating. Leonid Andreich has taken a position in the bank, six thousand a year . . .

ANYA

(In the doorway) Mama asks you to wait till she leaves before you cut down the orchard.

TROFIMOV

You might indeed show a bit more tact . . . *(Exits through front hall)*

LOPAKHIN

All right, all right . . . What's with them, really! *(Exits after him)*

ANYA

Has Firs been sent to the hospital?

YASHA

I told them this morning. I suppose it's been done.

ANYA

(To Epikhodov, who passes through the room) Semyon Panteleich, please find out if Firs has been sent to the hospital.

YASHA

(Offended) I told Egor this morning. Why ask ten times!

EPIKHODOV

The long-lived Firs, in my definitive opinion, is not fit for repair. He ought to join his ancestors. And I can only envy him. *(Steps on something hard)* Well, there, of course. I just knew it. *(Exits)*

YASHA

(Mockingly) Two-and-twenty Catastrophes . . .

VARYA

(Behind the door) Has Firs been taken to the hospital?

ANYA

Yes, he has.

VARYA

Why didn't they take the letter for the doctor?

ANYA

They'll have to send it after him . . . *(Exits)*

VARYA

(From the next room) Where's Yasha? Tell him his mother has come and wants to say good-bye to him.

YASHA

(Waves his hand) I'm at the end of my patience!

Dunyasha has been fussing with the luggage all the while; now that Yasha is left alone, she goes up to him.

DUNYASHA

You might look at me at least once, Yasha. You're leaving . . . you're abandoning me . . . *(Weeps and throws herself on his neck)*

YASHA

Why cry? *(Drinks champagne)* In six days I'll be back in Paris. Tomorrow we'll get on the express and go rolling off, and that's

the last you'll see of us. I can hardly believe it. Veev la France! . . .
I can't live here, it's not for me . . . that's how it is. I've had enough
of looking at this ignorance. *(Drinks champagne)* Why cry? If you
behaved yourself properly, you wouldn't cry.

DUNYASHA

(Looks in a small mirror and powders her nose) Send me a letter
from Paris. I loved you, Yasha, I loved you so!

YASHA

They're coming. *(Busies himself with the suitcases, humming softly)*
"Oh, wilt thou grasp the stirrings of my soul . . ."

Lyubov Andreevna, Gaev, Anya and Charlotta Ivanovna enter.

GAEV

We ought to go. There's not much time left. *(Looking at Yasha)*
Who smells of herring?

LYUBOV ANDREEVNA

So, in about five minutes let's get into the carriages . . . *(Gazes
around the room)* Good-bye, dear house, old grandfather. Winter will pass, spring will come, and you'll be no more, you'll be
torn down. These walls have seen so much! *(Kisses her daughter
warmly)* You're beaming, my treasure, your dear eyes are sparkling
like two diamonds. So you're glad? Very glad?

ANYA

Very! It's the beginning of a new life, mama!

GAEV

In fact, all's well now. Before the sale of the cherry orchard, we
were all upset, we suffered, but once the question was decided
finally, irrevocably, we all calmed down, became cheerful even . . .
I'm a bank official, a financier . . . yellow into the side . . . and you,
Lyuba, are looking better, after all, no doubt about it.

LYUBOV ANDREEVNA

Yes. My nerves are better, it's true.

She is given her hat and coat.

I sleep well. Carry my things out, Yasha. It's time. *(To Anya)* My dear girl, we'll see each other soon . . . I'm going to Paris, I'll live there on the money your great-aunt from Yaroslavl sent to buy the estate—long live our great-aunt!—and that money won't last long. Well, uncle has got a position in a bank . . .

ANYA

You'll come back soon, mama, very soon . . . won't you? I'll study, pass the exams at school, and then I'll work, I'll help you. We'll read all kinds of books together, mama . . . Won't we? *(Kisses her mother's hands)* We'll read in the autumn evenings, we'll read lots of books, and a new, wonderful world will open before us . . . *(Dreamily)* Come back, mama . . .

LYUBOV ANDREEVNA

I will, my jewel. *(Embraces Anya)*

Lopakhin enters. Charlotta softly hums a little song.

GAEV

Happy Charlotta: she's singing!

CHARLOTTA

(Picks up a bundle which looks like a swaddled baby) Bye-o, baby, bye-o . . .

Sound of a baby crying: "Wah, wah!"

Hush, my sweet, my dear little boy.

"Wah! Wah!"

I'm so sorry for you! *(Throws the bundle back where it had been)*
So, find me a position, please. I can't go on like this.

LOPAKHIN

We will, Charlotta Ivanovna, don't worry.

GAEV

Everybody's abandoning us, Varya's leaving . . . we've suddenly
become unnecessary.

CHARLOTTA

I've got nowhere to live in your town . . . I have to leave . . . *(Hums)*
Who cares . . .

Pishchik enters.

LOPAKHIN

A wonder of nature! . . .

PISHCHIK

(Breathless) Oh, let me catch my breath . . . I'm worn out . . . My
esteemed friends . . . Give me some water . . .

GAEV

In need of money, no doubt? Your humble servant, I'll get out of
harm's way . . . *(Exits)*

PISHCHIK

Haven't been here for quite some time . . . most beautiful lady . . .
(To Lopakhin) So you're here . . . glad to see you . . . a man of vast
intellect . . . here . . . take this . . . *(Hands Lopakhin money)* Four
hundred roubles . . . I still owe you eight hundred and forty . . .

LOPAKHIN

(Shrugs his shoulders in bewilderment) Am I dreaming? . . . Where'd
you get it?

PISHCHIK

Wait . . . I'm hot . . . A most extraordinary event . . . Some English-men came to me and found some sort of white clay in my soil . . . *(To Lyubov Andreevna)* Four hundred for you . . . my beautiful, astonishing lady . . . *(Hands her the money)* The rest later. *(Drinks water)* Just now a young man on the train was telling how some . . . great philosopher supposedly recommends jumping off the roof . . . "Jump!" he says. That's all there is to it. Water!

LOPAKHIN

Who are these Englishmen?

PISHCHIK

I leased them the plot with the clay for twenty-four years . . . *(With surprise)* Imagine that! And now, forgive me, no time . . . I must gal-lop on . . . I'm going to Znoikov . . . to Kardamonov . . . I owe them all . . . *(Drinks)* Be well . . . I'll come by on Thursday . . .

LYUBOV ANDREEVNA

We're moving to town now, and tomorrow I'm going abroad . . .

PISHCHIK

What's that? *(Alarmed)* Why to town? Aha, I see, the furniture . . . suitcases . . . Well, never mind . . . *(Through tears)* Never mind . . . They're people of vast intelligence . . . these Englishmen . . . Never mind . . . I wish you all happiness . . . God will help you . . . Never mind . . . Everything in this world must come to an end . . . *(Kisses Lyubov Andreevna's hand)* And when the news reaches you that I've met my end, remember this old horse and say: "Once upon a time there lived a . . . a . . . Simeonov-Pishchik . . . a horse . . . God rest his soul" . . . Most wonderful weather . . . Yes . . . *(Exits, but comes back at once and says from the doorway)* Dashenka sends her greetings! *(Exits)*

LYUBOV ANDREEVNA

Now we can go. I'm leaving with two worries. The first is the ailing Firs. *(Glancing at her watch)* Another five minutes . . .

ANYA

Firs has been sent to the hospital, mama. Yasha sent him this morning.

LYUBOV ANDREEVNA

My second grief is—Varya. She's used to getting up early and working, and now, without work, she's like a fish out of water. The poor thing's grown thin, pale, and she keeps crying . . .

Pause.

As you know very well, Ermolai Alexeich, I dreamed . . . of giving her away to you, and it did look as if you were going to marry her. *(Whispers to Anya, who nods to Charlotta, and both exit)* She loves you, you're fond of her, and I don't know, I don't know why it is that you seem to avoid each other. I don't understand!

LOPAKHIN

I admit, I don't understand it either. It's all somehow strange . . . If there's still time, I'm ready right now . . . Let's finish it at once— and be done!

LYUBOV ANDREEVNA

Excellent. It will only take a minute. I'll call her at once . . .

LOPAKHIN

There's champagne, as it happens. *(Looks at the glasses)* They're empty. Somebody drank it all.

Yasha coughs.

That's what's known as slurping it up . . .

LYUBOV ANDREEVNA

(Animated) Wonderful. We'll step outside . . . Yasha, *allez!* I'll call her . . . *(Through the door)* Varya, drop everything and come here. Come! *(Exits with Yasha)*

LOPAKHIN

(Glancing at his watch) Hm, yes . . .

Pause.

   Restrained laughter and whispering behind the door; Varya finally enters.

VARYA

(Examining the luggage for a long time) Strange, I just can't find . . .

LOPAKHIN

What are you looking for?

VARYA

I packed it myself and now I don't remember.

Pause.

LOPAKHIN

Where will you be going now, Varvara Mikhailovna?

VARYA

Me? To the Ragulins' . . . We've arranged for me to look after their household . . . as housekeeper or something.

LOPAKHIN

In Yashnevo, isn't it? Some fifty miles from here.

Pause.

So life in this house is over . . .

VARYA

(Looking over the luggage) Where is that . . . Maybe I packed it in the trunk . . . Yes, life is over in this house . . . there won't be any more . . .

LOPAKHIN

And I'm about to leave for Kharkov . . . on this train. There's a lot to do. I'm leaving Epikhodov here . . . I've hired him.

VARYA

Well, there!

LOPAKHIN

Last year around this time it was already snowing, if you remember, and now it's clear, calm, sunny. Only it's cold . . . Three below.

VARYA

I didn't look . . .

Pause.

Besides, our thermometer's broken . . .

Pause.
Voice through the door from outside: "Ermolai Alexeich!"

LOPAKHIN

(As if he had long been waiting for that call) Coming! *(Quickly exits)*

Varya sits down on the floor, her head on a bundle of clothes, and softly weeps.
The door opens, Lyubov Andreevna enters cautiously.

LYUBOV ANDREEVNA

Well?

Pause.

We must go.

VARYA

(No longer weeping, her tears wiped) Yes, it's time, mama. I'll hurry off to the Ragulins' today, if only I'm not late for the train . . .

LYUBOV ANDREEVNA

(Through the door) Anya, put your coat on!

Anya enters, then Gaev and Charlotta Ivanovna. Gaev is wearing a warm coat with a hood. Servants and coachmen gather. Epikhodov busies himself with the luggage.

Now we can be on our way.

ANYA

(Joyfully) On our way!

GAEV

My friends, my dear, good friends! In leaving this house forever, how can I be silent, how can I keep from expressing, by way of farewell, the feelings that now fill my whole being . . . My friends, you who have deeply felt, just as I have, who know . . .

ANYA

(Entreating) Oh, uncle!

VARYA

Dearest uncle, don't!

GAEV

Double the yellow into the side . . . I'll be quiet . . .

Trofimov enters, then Lopakhin.

TROFIMOV

Well, ladies and gentlemen, it's time to go!

LOPAKHIN

Epikhodov, my coat!

LYUBOV ANDREEVNA

I'll sit down for one little minute more. It's as if I never saw before what sort of walls this house has, what sort of ceilings, and now I look at them greedily, with such tender love . . .

GAEV

I remember when I was six years old, sitting in this window at Pentecost and watching my father walk to church . . .

LYUBOV ANDREEVNA

Has all the luggage been taken out?

LOPAKHIN

It seems so. *(To Epikhodov, putting on his coat)* Epikhodov, see that everything's in order.

EPIKHODOV

(Speaking in a husky voice) Don't you worry, Ermolai Alexeich!

LOPAKHIN

What's wrong with your voice?

EPIKHODOV

I just took a drink of water and swallowed something.

YASHA

(Laughs into his fist) Ignorance . . .

LYUBOV ANDREEVNA

We'll leave—and there won't be a soul left here . . .

LOPAKHIN

Till spring.

VARYA

(Pulls an umbrella from a bundle, looks as if she's raising it to hit him; Lopakhin jumps away) Don't worry, don't worry . . . I wasn't going to . . .

TROFIMOV

Let's get into the carriages, ladies and gentlemen . . . It's time! The train's about to come!

VARYA

Here are your galoshes, Petya, next to this suitcase. *(In tears)* They're so dirty, so old . . .

TROFIMOV

(Putting on his galoshes) Let's go, ladies and gentlemen!

GAEV

(Very confused, afraid he will start weeping) The train . . . the station . . . *Croisé* into the side . . . double the white into the corner . . .

LYUBOV ANDREEVNA

Let's go!

LOPAKHIN

Everybody here? Nobody in there? *(Locks the side door to the left)* Things have been put in storage there, it's got to be locked up. Let's go! . . .

ANYA

Good-bye, house! Good-bye, old life!

TROFIMOV

Hello, new life! . . . *(Exits with Anya)*

Varya looks around the room and exits unhurriedly. Exit Yasha and Charlotta with her little dog.

ANTON CHEKHOV

LOPAKHIN
Till spring, then. Step out, ladies and gentlemen . . . Bye-bye! . . .
(Exits)

Lyubov Andreevna and Gaev remain alone. As if they had been waiting for it, they throw themselves on each other's necks and weep restrainedly, softly, for fear of being heard.

GAEV
(In despair) My sister, my sister . . .

LYUBOV ANDREEVNA
Oh, my dear, my tender, my beautiful orchard! . . . My life, my youth, my happiness, good-bye! . . . Good-bye! . . .

Anya's voice: "Mama! . . ." Trofimov's voice: "Yoo-hoo! . . ."

(Weeps) I must cry softly . . . they'll hear me . . . One last look at these walls, these windows . . . Our late mother liked to walk about in this room . . .

GAEV
My sister, my sister! . . .

Anya's voice: "Mama! . . ." Trofimov's voice: "Yoo-hoo! . . ."

LYUBOV ANDREEVNA
We're coming! . . .

They exit.
　　The stage is empty. There is the sound of keys turning in both doors, then of the carriages driving off. Then all is quiet. Amidst the quiet there is the muted noise of an axe striking wood, sounding solitary and sad. Footsteps are heard. From the door to the right, Firs appears. He is dressed as usual in a jacket and white waistcoat, with slippers on his feet. He is ill.

FIRS

(Goes to the door, tries the handle) Locked. They've gone ... *(Sits down on the sofa)* Forgot about me ... Never mind ... I'll sit here for a bit ... I'll sit ... It's good, it's nice like this ... Leonid Andreich probably didn't put on his fur coat, went just in his topcoat ... *(Preoccupied sigh)* I didn't check on him ... Green youth! *(Mutters something incomprehensible)* Life's gone by, as if I never lived. *(Lies down)* I'll lie down for a bit ... You've got no strength, you've got nothing left, nothing ... Eh, you ... blunderhead! ... *(Lies still)*

A distant sound, as if from the sky, the sound of a breaking string, dying away, sad. Silence ensues, and the only thing heard is an axe striking wood far off in the orchard.
    Curtain.

THE
CHERRY
ORCHARD

1904 Moscow Art Theatre Script

Characters

LYUBÓV ANDRÉEVNA RANÉVSKAYA (Lyúba), a landowner

ÁNYA (Ánechka), her daughter, seventeen years old

VÁRYA (Varvára Mikháilovna), her adopted daughter, twenty-four years old

LEONÍD ANDRÉEVICH GÁEV (Lyónya), Ranevskaya's brother

ERMOLÁI ALEXÉEVICH LOPÁKHIN (Alexéich), a merchant

PYÓTR SERGÉEVICH TROFÍMOV (Pétya), a student

BORÍS BORÍSOVICH SIMEÓNOV-PÍSHCHIK, a landowner

CHARLÓTTA IVÁNOVNA [no last name], a governess

SEMYÓN PANTELÉEVICH EPIKHÓDOV, a clerk

DUNYÁSHA (Avdótya Fyódorvna Kozoédova), a maid

FIRS (Nikolaevich), a servant, eighty-seven years old

YÁSHA, a young servant

A PASSERBY

THE STATIONMASTER

A POSTAL CLERK

GUESTS, SERVANTS

The action takes place on L. A. Ranevskaya's estate.

ACT ONE

A room which is still called the nursery. One of the doors leads to Anya's room. Daybreak, the sun will rise soon. It is already May, the cherry trees are in bloom, but it is chilly. There is a morning frost in the orchard. The windows in the room are shut.

Dunyasha enters with a candle and Lopakhin with a book in his hand.

LOPAKHIN

The train's come, thank God. What time is it?

DUNYASHA

Going on two. *(Blows out the candle)* It's already light.

LOPAKHIN

How late does that make the train? A couple of hours at least. *(Yawns and stretches)* I'm a fine one, too! Made a fool of myself! Came here on purpose to meet them at the station, and slept right through it . . . Sat down and fell asleep. A shame . . . You might have waked me up.

DUNYASHA

I thought you left. *(Listens)* There, I think it's them.

LOPAKHIN

(Listens) No . . . They've got to pick up the luggage and all that . . .

Pause.

Lyubov Andreevna's been living abroad for five years. I don't know what she's like now . . . She's a good person. Easy, simple. I remember when I was a kid of about fifteen, my late father—he kept a shop then, here in the village—punched me in the face with his fist. My nose bled . . . We had come here to the yard together for some reason, and he was a bit drunk. Lyubov Andreevna, I remember it like today, still a young thing, so slender, she led me to the washstand, here, in this same room, in the nursery. "Don't cry, peasant-boy," she says, "it'll go away by your wedding day . . ."

Pause.

Peasant-boy . . . True, my father was a peasant, but here I am in a white waistcoat and yellow shoes. A pig in the parlor . . . Oh, I'm rich all right, I've got lots of money, but if you really look into it, I'm as peasant as a peasant can be . . . *(Leafs through the book)* I'm reading this book and don't understand a thing. I fell asleep reading it.

Pause.

DUNYASHA

And the dogs didn't sleep all night. They can sense the masters are coming.

LOPAKHIN

Dunyasha, why are you so—

DUNYASHA

My hands are trembling. I feel faint.

LOPAKHIN

You're much too pampered, Dunyasha. You dress like a young lady, and do your hair up, too. It's not right. Remember who you are.

Epikhodov enters with a bouquet. He wears a jacket and brightly polished boots that creak loudly. He drops the bouquet as he enters.

EPIKHODOV

(Picking up the bouquet) The gardener sent it. He says to put it in the dining room. *(He hands the bouquet to Dunyasha)*

LOPAKHIN

And bring me some kvass.

DUNYASHA

Yes, sir. *(Exits)*

EPIKHODOV

There's a morning frost, three below, and the cherry trees are all in bloom. I cannot approve of our climate. *(He sighs)* I cannot. Our climate cannot aptly contribute. And allow me to append another thing, Ermolai Alexeich. I bought myself some boots two days ago, and, I venture to assure you, they creak so much it's quite impossible. Can I grease them with something?

LOPAKHIN

Leave me alone. I'm sick of you.

EPIKHODOV

Every day some new catastrophe befalls me. And I don't complain, I'm used to it, I even smile.

Dunyasha enters, serves Lopakhin his kvass.

I'm leaving. *(He bumps into a chair, which falls over)* There . . . *(As if triumphantly)* There, you see. What a happenstance, by the way, if you'll pardon the expression . . . It's simply even remarkable! *(Exits)*

DUNYASHA

And I must tell you, Ermolai Alexeich, Epikhodov has proposed to me.

LOPAKHIN

Ah!

DUNYASHA

I really don't know how to . . . He's nice enough, only sometimes he gets to talking so you don't understand a thing. It's good, it's sensitive, only it's incomprehensible. I even seem to like him. He's madly in love with me. He's an unlucky man, every day there's something. They tease him about it here, they call him "Two-and-twenty Catastrophes."

LOPAKHIN

(Listens) There, I think it's them . . .

DUNYASHA

It's them! What's the matter with me . . . I've gone cold all over.

LOPAKHIN

It's really them. Let's go and meet them. Will she recognize me? Five years we haven't seen each other.

DUNYASHA

(Agitated) I'm going to faint . . . Oh, I'm fainting!

The sound of two carriages driving up to the house. Lopakhin and Dunyasha exit quickly. The stage is empty. Noise starts in the adjacent rooms. Firs, who went to meet Lyubov Andreevna, hastily crosses the stage, leaning on a stick; he is wearing old-fashioned livery and a top hat. He says something to himself, but it is impossible to make out a single word. The noise backstage keeps growing louder. A voice says: "Let's go through here . . ." Lyubov Andreevna, Anya and Charlotta Ivanovna with a little dog on a leash enter, dressed in traveling clothes. They are followed by Varya, wearing a coat and shawl, Gaev, Simeonov-Pishchik, Lopakhin, Dunyasha with a bundle and an umbrella, servants with the luggage. They all walk through the room.

ANYA

Let's go through here. Do you remember what room this is, mama?

LYUBOV ANDREEVNA

(Joyfully, through tears) The nursery!

VARYA

It's so cold! My hands are freezing. *(To Lyubov Andreevna)* Your rooms, the white one and the violet one, have stayed just as they were, mama.

LYUBOV ANDREEVNA

The nursery, my dear, beautiful room . . . I slept here when I was little . . . *(Weeps)* And it's as if I'm little now . . . *(She kisses her brother, then Varya, then her brother again)* And Varya's the same as before, looking like a nun. And I recognize Dunyasha . . . *(She kisses Dunyasha)*

GAEV

The train was two hours late. How about that, eh? How about that for efficiency?

CHARLOTTA

(To Pishchik) My dog eats nuts also.

PISHCHIK

(Surprised) Imagine that!

Exit all but Anya and Dunyasha.

DUNYASHA

How we waited . . . *(She takes Anya's coat and hat)*

ANYA

I didn't sleep for four nights on the train . . . I'm so chilled now.

DUNYASHA

You left during the Great Lent, there was snow then, it was freezing, and now? My dear! *(Laughs, kisses her)* How I waited for you, my joy, my angel . . . I'll tell you now, I can't wait . . .

ANYA

(Listlessly) Here we go again . . .

DUNYASHA

The clerk Epikhodov proposed to me after Easter.

ANYA

That's all you ever . . . *(Straightens her hair)* I lost all my hairpins . . . *(She is very tired, even staggers a little)*

DUNYASHA

I just don't know what to think. He loves me, he loves me so!

ANYA

(Looks through the door to her room, tenderly) My room, my windows, as if I never left. I'm home! Tomorrow morning I'll get up and run out to the orchard . . . Oh, if only I could fall asleep! I didn't sleep all the way, I was worn out with worry.

DUNYASHA

Pyotr Sergeich arrived two days ago.

ANYA

(Joyfully) Petya!

DUNYASHA

He's asleep in the bathhouse. That's where he's staying. I'm afraid to inconvenience them, he says. *(Glancing at her pocket watch)*

I ought to wake him up, but Varvara Mikhailovna told me not to. Don't wake him up, she says.

Varya enters with a bunch of keys hanging from her belt.

VARYA

Dunyasha, coffee, quickly . . . Mama's asking for coffee.

DUNYASHA

Right away. *(Exits)*

VARYA

Well, thank God you've come. You're home again. *(Caressingly)* My darling has come! My beauty has come!

ANYA

I've been through a lot.

VARYA

I can imagine!

ANYA

I left during Holy Week. It was cold then. Charlotta talked all the way, and played card tricks. Why on earth did you stick me with Charlotta . . .

VARYA

You couldn't have gone alone, darling. Not at seventeen!

ANYA

We arrive in Paris. It's cold there, snowy. My French is awful. Mama lives on the fifth floor, I go in, there are some French people there, ladies, an old padre with a book, cigarette smoke, cheerless. I suddenly felt so sorry for mama, so sorry, I took her head in my arms, pressed it to me, and couldn't let go. After that mama just kept hugging me and crying . . .

VARYA

(Through tears) Don't tell me, don't . . .

ANYA

She had already sold her house near Menton, and she had nothing left, nothing. I also didn't have a kopeck left, we barely made it home. And mama doesn't understand! We sit down to dinner in the station and she orders the most expensive things and tips the waiter a rouble. Then there's Charlotta. Yasha also orders something. It's just awful. Mama has this servant Yasha, we've brought him with us . . .

VARYA

I saw the scoundrel.

ANYA

Well, so, how are things? Have we paid the interest?

VARYA

Far from it.

ANYA

My God, my God . . .

VARYA

They'll put the estate up for sale in August . . .

ANYA

My God . . .

LOPAKHIN

(Peeks through the door and moos) Meu-u-h. *(Exits)*

VARYA

(Through tears) Oh, I could give it to him . . . *(Shakes her fist)*

ANYA

(Embraces Varya, softly) Varya, has he proposed? *(Varya shakes her head no)* But he does love you . . . Why don't you have a talk? What are you waiting for?

VARYA

I don't think it'll come to anything. He has a lot to do, he can't be bothered with me . . . he pays no attention. Enough of him, it's hard for me to look at him . . . Everybody talks about us getting married, everybody congratulates me, but in fact there's nothing, it's all like a dream . . . *(In a different tone)* Your brooch looks like a little bee.

ANYA

(Sadly) Mama bought it for me. *(Goes to her room, talks gaily, childishly)* In Paris I flew in a hot-air balloon.

VARYA

My darling's come home! My beauty's come home!

Dunyasha has now returned with the coffee pot and is preparing coffee.

(Standing by the door) I go around all day, darling, looking after the house, and I keep dreaming. To see you married to a rich man. I'd be at peace then, and I'd take myself to a convent, then to Kiev . . . to Moscow, and go around like that to all the holy places . . . go on and on. What blessedness!

ANYA

The birds are singing in the orchard. What time is it?

VARYA

Must be nearly three. It's time you went to bed, darling. *(Going into Anya's room)* What blessedness!

Yasha enters with a lap blanket and a traveling bag.

YASHA

(Walks across the stage, asks mincingly) May I pass through here, miss?

DUNYASHA

I'd never have recognized you, Yasha. See what's become of you abroad!

YASHA

Hm . . . And who are you?

DUNYASHA

I was only so high when you left . . . *(Shows height from the floor)* Dunyasha, Fyodor Kozoedov's daughter. Don't you remember?!

YASHA

Hm . . . Cute little cucumber! *(Glances around and embraces her; she cries out and drops a saucer. Yasha quickly exits)*

VARYA

(In the doorway, displeased) What's going on here?

DUNYASHA

(Through tears) I broke a saucer . . .

VARYA

That means good luck.

ANYA

(Coming out of her room) We should warn mama that Petya's here . . .

VARYA

I gave orders not to wake him up.

ANYA

(Pensively) Father died six years ago. A month later my brother Grisha drowned in the river—a pretty seven-year-old boy. Mama couldn't bear it, she left, left without looking back . . . *(Shudders)* How well I understand her, if only she knew!

Pause.

And Petya Trofimov was Grisha's tutor, he might remind her of . . .

Firs enters wearing a jacket and white waistcoat.

FIRS

(Approaches the coffee pot, preoccupied) The lady will have coffee here . . . *(Puts on white gloves)* Is the coffee ready? *(Sternly, to Dunyasha)* You! Where's the cream?

DUNYASHA

Oh, my God . . . *(Exits quickly)*

FIRS

(Fussing over the coffee pot) Eh, you blunderhead . . . *(Mutters to himself)* So they're home from Paris . . . Used to be the master went to Paris . . . by horse and carriage . . . *(Laughs)*

VARYA

What is it, Firs?

FIRS

If you please. *(Joyfully)* My lady has come home! How I've waited! Now I can die . . . *(Weeps from joy)*

Lyubov Andreevna, Gaev, Lopakhin and Simeonov-Pishchik enter. Simeonov-Pishchik is wearing a sleeveless jacket of fine broadcloth and balloon trousers.
Gaev, as he enters, makes the motions of playing billiards.

LYUBOV ANDREEVNA

How does it go? Let me remember . . . Yellow into the corner! Double into the side!

GAEV

Cut shot into the corner! Once upon a time you and I slept in this room, sister, and now I'm already fifty-one, strangely enough . . .

LOPAKHIN

Yes, time flies.

GAEV

Whoso?

LOPAKHIN

I said, time flies.

GAEV

It smells of cheap cologne here.

ANYA

I'm going to bed. Good night, mama. *(Kisses her mother)*

LYUBOV ANDREEVNA

My beloved little baby. *(Kisses her hands)* Are you glad to be home? I can't get over it.

ANYA

Good-bye, uncle.

GAEV

(Kisses her face and hands) God bless you. You're so much like your mother! *(To his sister)* You were exactly the same at her age, Lyuba.

Anya gives her hand to Lopakhin and Pishchik, exits, and closes the door behind her.

LYUBOV ANDREEVNA

She's very tired.

PISHCHIK

It must have been a long trip.

VARYA

(To Lopakhin and Pishchik) Well, gentlemen? It's nearly three, don't wear out your welcome.

LYUBOV ANDREEVNA

(Laughs) You're still the same, Varya. *(Pulls her to herself and kisses her)* I'll have my coffee, then we'll all go.

Firs puts a little cushion under her feet.

Thank you, dearest. I've grown used to coffee. I drink it day and night. Thank you, my dear old man. *(She kisses Firs)*

VARYA

I'll see if they've brought all the things . . . *(Exits)*

LYUBOV ANDREEVNA

Can it be me sitting here? *(Laughs)* I want to jump around, wave my arms. *(Covers her face with her hands)* What if I'm asleep! God is my witness, I love my country, love it tenderly, I couldn't look out of the train, I kept crying. *(Through tears)* I must have my coffee, though. Thank you, Firs, thank you, my dear old man. I'm so glad you're still alive.

FIRS

Two days ago.

GAEV

He's hard of hearing.

LOPAKHIN

I've got to leave for Kharkov at five this morning. What a shame!
I wanted to have a look at you, to talk a little . . . You're as magnificent as ever.

PISHCHIK

(Breathing heavily) Even got prettier . . . Dressed up Parisian-
style . . . really bowls me over . . .

LOPAKHIN

Your brother, Leonid Andreevich here, goes around saying I'm a
boor, a money-grubber, but it's decidedly all the same to me. Let
him talk. All I want is for you to believe me like before, that your
astonishing, moving eyes look at me like before. Merciful God! My
father was your grandfather's serf, and your father's, but you, you
personally, once did so much for me that I've forgotten all that and
love you like one of my own . . . more than one of my own.

LYUBOV ANDREEVNA

I can't sit still, I just can't . . . *(Jumps up and paces about in great
excitement)* I won't survive this joy . . . Laugh at me, I'm stupid . . .
My own little bookcase . . . *(Kisses the bookcase)* My little table.

GAEV

Nanny died while you were away.

LYUBOV ANDREEVNA

(Sits down and drinks her coffee) Yes, God rest her soul. They
wrote to me.

GAEV

And Anastasy died. Cross-eyed Petrushka left me and now lives
in town at the police chief's. *(Takes a box of fruit drops from his
pocket, sucks on one)*

PISHCHIK

My daughter, Dashenka . . . sends you her greetings . . .

LOPAKHIN

I would like to tell you something very pleasant and cheerful. *(Looks at his watch)* I've got to go now, there's no time to talk . . . well, so, in two or three words. As you already know, your cherry orchard is going to be sold off to pay your debts, the auction will be on August twenty-second, but don't worry, my dear, rest easy, there's a way out . . . Here's my plan. Please pay attention! Your estate is located only fifteen miles from town, the railroad now passes nearby, and if the cherry orchard and the land by the river were broken up into lots and leased out for building summer houses, you'd have an income of at least twenty-five thousand a year.

GAEV

Excuse me, but that's nonsense!

LYUBOV ANDREEVNA

I don't quite understand you, Ermolai Alexeich.

LOPAKHIN

You'll charge the summer people a yearly rent of at least ten roubles per acre, and if you advertise right now, I'll bet anything you like that by autumn you won't have a single free scrap left, it'll all be snapped up. In short, congratulations, you're saved. The location's wonderful, the river's deep. Though, of course, there'll have to be some clearing away, some cleaning up . . . for instance, you'll have to pull down all the old buildings, like this house, which is no longer good for anything, and chop down the old cherry orchard . . .

LYUBOV ANDREEVNA

Chop it down? My dear, forgive me, but you understand nothing. If there's one thing in the whole province that's interesting, even remarkable, it's our cherry orchard.

LOPAKHIN

The only remarkable thing about this orchard is that it's very big. It produces cherries once in two years, and there's nothing to do with them, nobody buys them.

GAEV

This orchard is even mentioned in the *Encyclopedia*.

LOPAKHIN

(Glancing at his watch) If we don't come up with anything and don't reach any decision, both the cherry orchard and the entire estate will be sold at auction on August twenty-second. Make up your minds! There's no other way out, I swear to you. None. None.

FIRS

In the old days, forty or fifty years ago, the cherries were dried, bottled, made into juice, preserves, and we used to . . .

GAEV

Be quiet, Firs.

FIRS

And we used to send cartloads of dried cherries to Moscow and Kharkov. The money we made! And those dried cherries were soft, juicy, sweet, fragrant . . . They knew a way . . .

LYUBOV ANDREEVNA

And where is that way now?

FIRS

Forgotten. Nobody remembers it.

PISHCHIK

(To Lyubov Andreevna) How are things in Paris? Eh? Eat any frogs?

LYUBOV ANDREEVNA

No . . . crocodiles.

PISHCHIK

Imagine that . . .

LOPAKHIN

Before there were just gentry and peasants here, but now these summer people have appeared. All the towns, even the smallest ones, are surrounded by summer houses now. And it's safe to say that in some twenty years the summer people will multiply incredibly. Right now they only drink tea on their balconies, but it may well happen that they take to farming their little acres, and then your cherry orchard will become happy, rich, luxuriant . . .

GAEV

(Indignantly) What nonsense!

Varya and Yasha enter.

VARYA

Two telegrams came for you, mama. *(Chooses a key and with a ringing noise opens the old bookcase)* Here they are.

LYUBOV ANDREEVNA

From Paris. *(Tears up the telegrams without reading them)* I'm through with Paris . . .

GAEV

Do you know how old this bookcase is, Lyuba? Last week I pulled out the lower drawer, I look, there are numbers burnt into it. This bookcase was made exactly a hundred years ago. How about that? Eh? We could celebrate its jubilee. It's an inanimate object, but still, all the same, it's a bookcase.

PISHCHIK

(Surprised) A hundred years . . . Imagine that . . .

GAEV

Yes . . . That's something . . . *(Pats the bookcase)* Dear, much-esteemed bookcase! I hail your existence, which for more than a hundred years now has been intent upon the bright ideals of justice

and the good. Your silent summons to fruitful work has never slackened in those hundred years, maintaining courage in the generations
of our family, *(He becomes tearful)* faith in a better future, and fostering in us the ideals of the good and of social consciousness.

Pause.

LOPAKHIN

Hm, yes . . .

LYUBOV ANDREEVNA

You're the same as ever, Lyonya.

GAEV

(Slightly embarrassed) Carom into the right corner! Cut shot into
the side!

LOPAKHIN

(Glancing at his watch) Well, time to go.

YASHA

(Offering Lyubov Andreevna medicine) Maybe you'll take your pills
now . . .

PISHCHIK

No need to take medicines, my dear . . . they do no harm, and no
good . . . Let me have them . . . my most respected lady. *(Takes the
pills, pours them into his palm, blows on them, puts them in his
mouth, and washes them down with kvass)* There!

LYUBOV ANDREEVNA

(Frightened) You're out of your mind!

PISHCHIK

I took all the pills.

LOPAKHIN

A bottomless pit.

Everybody laughs.

FIRS

The gentleman came here during Holy Week and ate half a bucket of pickles ... *(Mutters something)*

LYUBOV ANDREEVNA

What's he saying?

VARYA

He's been muttering like that for three years now. We're used to it.

YASHA

On the decline.

Charlotta Ivanovna, in a white dress, very thin, tightly corseted, with a lorgnette at her waist, walks across the stage.

LOPAKHIN

Forgive me, Charlotta Ivanovna, I haven't greeted you yet. *(Tries to kiss her hand)*

CHARLOTTA

(Pulling her hand back) If I allow you to kiss my hand, then you'll want to kiss my elbow, then my shoulder ...

LOPAKHIN

I have no luck today.

Everybody laughs.

Charlotta Ivanovna, show us a trick.

LYUBOV ANDREEVNA

Show us a trick, Charlotta!

CHARLOTTA

Not now. I wish to sleep. *(Exits)*

LOPAKHIN

See you in three weeks. *(Kisses Lyubov Andreevna's hand)* Good-bye for now. It's time. *(To Gaev)* Bye-bye. *(Exchanges kisses with Pishchik)* Bye-bye. *(Gives his hand to Varya, then to Firs and Yasha)* I don't feel like leaving. *(To Lyubov Andreevna)* Think it over about the summer houses, and if you decide to do it, let me know. I'll get you a loan of fifty thousand. Think seriously.

VARYA

(Angrily) Will you finally leave?!

LOPAKHIN

I'm leaving, I'm leaving . . . *(Exits)*

GAEV

A boor. *Pardon*, however . . . Varya's going to marry him, he's Varya's little suitor.

VARYA

You talk too much, uncle dear.

LYUBOV ANDREEVNA

Why, Varya, I'll be very glad. He's a good man.

PISHCHIK

A most worthy man . . . to tell the truth . . . And my Dashenka . . . also says that . . . says various things. *(Snores, then wakes up at once)* Anyhow, my most respected lady, lend me two hundred and forty roubles . . . to pay my mortgage interest tomorrow . . .

VARYA

(Frightened) We can't, we can't!

LYUBOV ANDREEVNA

I really have nothing at all.

PISHCHIK

It'll turn up. *(Laughs)* I never lose hope. That's it, I think, all is lost, I'm ruined, but, lo and behold—they build the railroad across my land, and . . . they pay me for it. Then, lo and behold, something else comes along, if not today then tomorrow . . . Dashenka wins two hundred thousand . . . on a lottery ticket.

LYUBOV ANDREEVNA

We've had our coffee, we can retire.

FIRS

(Brushing Gaev off, admonishingly) Again you've put on the wrong trousers. What am I to do with you!

VARYA

(Softly) Anya's asleep. *(Quietly opens the window)* The sun's up, it's not cold anymore. Look, mama: what wonderful trees! My God, what air! The starlings are singing!

GAEV

(Opens the other window) The orchard's all white. You haven't forgotten, Lyuba? That long alley goes straight on, straight on, like a belt stretched out. It glistens on moonlit nights. You remember? You haven't forgotten?

LYUBOV ANDREEVNA

(Looks out the window at the orchard) Oh, my childhood, my purity! I slept in this nursery, looked out from here at the orchard, happiness woke up with me every morning, and it was the same then as it is now, nothing has changed. *(Laughs joyfully)* All, all

white! Oh, my orchard! After dark, rainy autumn and cold winter, you are young again, full of happiness, the angels of heaven have not abandoned you ... If only the heavy stone could be lifted from my breast and shoulders, if only I could forget my past!

GAEV

Yes, and the orchard's going to be sold to pay our debts, strangely enough ...

LYUBOV ANDREEVNA

Look, my late mother is walking through the orchard ... in a white dress! *(Laughs joyfully)* It's her!

GAEV

Where?

VARYA

God help you, mama.

LYUBOV ANDREEVNA

No, there's nobody, I imagined it. To the right, at the turn towards the gazebo, there's a little white tree bending down ... It looks like a woman ...

Trofimov enters in a shabby student uniform, wearing glasses.

What an amazing orchard! Masses of white flowers, the blue sky ...

TROFIMOV

Lyubov Andreevna!

She turns to look at him.

I'll just say hello and leave at once. *(Kisses her hand warmly)* I was told to wait till morning, but I got impatient ...

Lyubov Andreevna looks at him, perplexed.

VARYA

(Through tears) It's Petya Trofimov . . .

TROFIMOV

Petya Trofimov, former tutor of your Grisha . . . Can I have changed so much?

Lyubov Andreevna embraces him and weeps quietly.

GAEV

(Embarrassed) Enough, enough now, Lyuba.

VARYA

(Weeps) I told you to wait till tomorrow, Petya.

LYUBOV ANDREEVNA

My Grisha . . . my little boy . . . Grisha . . . my son . . .

VARYA

There's no help for it, mama. It was God's will.

TROFIMOV

(Gently, through tears) There, there . . .

LYUBOV ANDREEVNA

(Weeps softly) My little boy died, he drowned . . . Why? Why, my friend? *(More softly)* Anya's asleep in there, and I talk so loudly . . . make noise . . . Well, so, Petya? How is it you've lost your looks? How is it you've aged so much?

TROFIMOV

A peasant woman on the train once called me a mangy mister.

LYUBOV ANDREEVNA

You were still a boy then, a sweet young student, and now—thin hair, glasses. Can it be you're still a student? *(Goes toward the door)*

TROFIMOV

Must be I'm an eternal student.

LYUBOV ANDREEVNA

(Kisses her brother, then Varya) Well, go to bed . . . You've aged, too, Leonid.

PISHCHIK

(Follows her) So, it's to bed now . . . Ah, this gout of mine. I'll stay here . . . Lyubov Andreevna, my dear heart, maybe, tomorrow morning . . . two hundred and forty roubles . . .

GAEV

He's still at it.

PISHCHIK

Two hundred and forty roubles . . . to pay the interest on the mortgage.

LYUBOV ANDREEVNA

I have no money, dear heart.

PISHCHIK

I'll pay it back, my dear . . . It's nothing . . .

LYUBOV ANDREEVNA

Well, all right, Leonid will give it to you . . . Give it to him, Leonid.

GAEV

Give it to him, hah! Good luck!

LYUBOV ANDREEVNA

What can we do? Give it to him . . . He needs it . . . He'll pay it back.

Lyubov Andreevna, Trofimov, Pishchik and Firs exit. Gaev, Varya and Yasha remain.

GAEV

My sister still has the habit of throwing money away. *(To Yasha)* Back off, my dear fellow, you smell of chicken.

YASHA

(With a smirk) And you, Leonid Andreich, are still the same as ever.

GAEV

Whoso? *(To Varya)* What did he say?

VARYA

(To Yasha) Your mother has come from the village. She's been sitting in the servants' quarters since yesterday, she wants to see you . . .

YASHA

As if I care!

VARYA

Shame on you!

YASHA

Who needs her. She could have come tomorrow. *(Exits)*

VARYA

Mama's still the same as ever, hasn't changed a bit. If she could, she'd give everything away.

GAEV

Yes . . .

Pause.

If a great many remedies are prescribed against an illness, it means the illness is incurable. I think, I wrack my brain, I have many remedies, a great many, which in fact means none. It would be nice to get an inheritance from somebody, it would be nice to have our Anya marry a very rich man, it would be nice to go to Yaroslavl and try our luck with our aunt, the countess. The aunt's very, very rich.

VARYA

(Weeps) If only God would help us!

GAEV

Stop blubbering. The aunt's very rich, but she doesn't like us. First of all, my sister married a lawyer, not a nobleman . . .

Anya appears in the doorway.

Didn't marry a nobleman, and can't be said to have behaved herself all that virtuously. She's good, kind, nice, I love her very much, but, whatever extenuating circumstances you think up, still, you must admit she's depraved. You can sense it in her slightest movement.

VARYA

(Whispers) Anya's in the doorway.

GAEV

Whoso?

Pause.

Extraordinary, something's gotten into my right eye . . . I can't see very well. And on Thursday, when I was in the circuit court . . .

Anya enters.

VARYA

Why aren't you asleep, Anya?

ANYA

I don't feel like sleeping. I can't.

GAEV

My tiny one. *(Kisses Anya's face and hands)* My child . . . *(Through tears)* You're not my niece, you're my angel, you're everything to me. Believe me, believe me . . .

ANYA

I believe you, uncle. Everybody loves you, respects you . . . but, uncle dear, you must be quiet, just be quiet. What was it you said about my mother, about your sister? Why did you say that?

GAEV

Right, right . . . *(Covers his face with his hands)* It's really terrible! My God! God, save me! And the speech I made earlier to the bookcase . . . so stupid! And it was only when I finished that I realized is was stupid.

VARYA

It's true, uncle dear, you must be quiet. Just be quiet, that's all.

ANYA

If you're quiet, you'll feel calmer yourself.

GAEV

I'm quiet. *(Kisses Anya's and Varya's hands)* I'm quiet. There's just this one thing. On Thursday I was in the circuit court, well, so a group gathered, a conversation began about this and that, one thing led to another, and it seems it may be possible to arrange a loan on credit to pay off the interest to the bank.

VARYA

If only God would help us!

GAEV

I'll go on Tuesday and talk it over again. *(To Varya)* Stop blubbering. *(To Anya)* Your mother will talk to Lopakhin; he certainly won't refuse her . . . And you, once you've rested, will go to Yaroslavl, to the countess, your great-aunt. So we'll attack from three directions—and it's in the bag. We'll pay the interest, I'm sure of it . . . *(Puts a fruit drop in his mouth)* I swear on my honor, on anything you like, the estate will not be sold! *(Excitedly)* I swear on my happiness. Here's my hand, call me a worthless, dishonorable man if I let it go up for auction! I swear on my whole being!

ANYA

(Her calm is restored, she is happy) You're so good, uncle, so intelligent! *(Embraces her uncle)* I'm at peace now! I'm at peace! I'm happy!

Firs enters.

FIRS

(Reproachfully) Leonid Andreich, have you no fear of God?! When are you going to bed?

GAEV

Right away, right away. You may go, Firs. Never mind, I'll undress myself. Well, children, bye-bye . . . Details tomorrow, but now go to bed. *(Kisses Anya and Varya)* I'm a man of the eighties . . . It's a time that's not much praised, but all I can say is, I've endured quite a lot for my convictions. It's not for nothing that the peasants love me. You've got to know the peasants! You've got to know how they . . .

ANYA

You're at it again, uncle!

VARYA

Quiet, uncle dear.

FIRS

(Crossly) Leonid Andreich!

GAEV

Coming, coming . . . Go to bed. Double bank shot into the side. Pot the clear ball . . . *(Exits. Firs trots along behind him)*

ANYA

I'm at peace now. I don't feel like going to Yaroslavl, I don't like my great-aunt, but all the same I'm at peace. Thanks to uncle. *(Sits down)*

VARYA

We must sleep. I'm going. There was some unpleasantness here while you were away. As you know, only the elderly servants live in the old servants' quarters: Efimyushka, Polya, Evstignei and Karp as well. They started letting some rascals spend the night with them—I said nothing. But then I hear they're spreading a rumor that I ordered them to be fed nothing but peas. Out of stinginess, you see . . . It's all Evstignei's doing . . . Very well, I think. In that case, I think, just you wait. I summon Evstignei . . . *(She yawns)* He comes . . . How is it, Evstignei, I say, fool that you are . . . *(Looks at Anya)* Anechka! . . .

Pause.

Asleep! . . . *(Takes Anya under the arm)* Let's go beddy-bye . . . Let's go! . . . *(Leads her)* My darling's asleep! Let's go! . . .

They start out. Far beyond the orchard, a shepherd is playing a pipe. Trofimov walks across the stage and, seeing Varya and Anya, stops.

VARYA

Shh . . . She's asleep . . . asleep . . . Let's go, my dearest.

ANYA

(Softly, half asleep) I'm so tired . . . these little bells . . . Uncle . . . dear . . . mama and uncle . . .

VARYA

Let's go, my dearest, let's go . . . *(They exit to Anya's room)*

TROFIMOV

(Tenderly) My sunshine! My springtime!

Curtain.

ACT TWO

A field. An old, lopsided, long-abandoned chapel, next to it a well, big stones that apparently once used to be tombstones, and an old bench. You can see the road to Gaev's estate. To the side, some poplars hover darkly: the cherry orchard begins there. In the distance a row of telegraph poles, and far away on the horizon a big town is vaguely outlined, which can be seen only in very fine, clear weather. The sun will set soon. Charlotta, Yasha and Dunyasha sit on the bench. Epikhodov stands by them and plays the guitar. They are all deep in thought. Charlotta wears an old visored cap; she has taken the gun from her shoulder and is adjusting the buckle on the sling.

CHARLOTTA

(Pensively) I have no real passport, I don't know how old I am, and I keep imagining I'm a young girl. When I was little, my father and mother went around to fairs and gave performances, very good ones. And I did the *salto mortale* and all sorts of tricks. And when father and mother died, a German lady took me in and began to teach me. Right. I grew up, then I went to be a governess. But

where I'm from and who I am, I don't know . . . Who my parents were, or whether they were even married . . . I don't know. *(Takes a cucumber from her pocket and eats)* I don't know anything.

Pause.

I'd like so much to talk to someone, but who is there . . . I have nobody.

EPIKHODOV

(Plays the guitar and sings) "What to me is the world and its noise, / what to me are friends and foes . . ." How nice to play the mandolin!

DUNYASHA

It's a guitar, not a mandolin. *(Looks in a little mirror and powders her nose)*

EPIKHODOV

For a madman in love it's a mandolin . . . *(Sings under his breath)* "So long as my heart knows the joys / of ardent love in all its throes . . ."

Yasha sings along.

CHARLOTTA

How terribly these people sing . . . yech! Like jackals.

DUNYASHA

(To Yasha) Still, you're so lucky to have traveled abroad.

YASHA

Yes, of course. I cannot help but agree with you. *(Yawns, then lights a cigar)*

EPIKHODOV

It's a known thing. Abroad everything has long been in full completeness.

YASHA

That goes without saying.

EPIKHODOV

I'm a cultivated man, I read all sorts of remarkable books, but I simply cannot understand where things are heading, and what in fact I want, to go on living or to shoot myself, but in any case, as a matter of fact, I always carry a revolver with me. Here it is . . . *(Shows the revolver)*

CHARLOTTA

Finished. I'll go now. *(Shoulders the gun)* You're a very smart man, Epikhodov, and a very scary one. Women must love you madly. Brr! *(Goes)* These smarties are all so stupid, I've got nobody to talk to . . . Alone, always alone, I have no one and . . . and who I am, why I am, there's no knowing . . . *(Exits unhurriedly)*

EPIKHODOV

As a matter of fact, regardless of other subjects, I must express about myself, by the way, that fate deals mercilessly with me, like a storm with a small boat. Supposing I'm mistaken, why then do I wake up this morning, for example, and see on my chest a spider of enormous proportions . . . This big. *(Shows with both hands)* Or I pick up a jug of kvass, so as to pour myself a drink, and there's something highly improper in it, like a cockroach.

Pause.

Have you read Buckle?

Pause.

I wish to trouble you, Avdotya Fyodorovna, with a couple of words.

DUNYASHA

Speak.

EPIKHODOV

It would be desirable for us to be alone . . . *(Sighs)*

DUNYASHA

(Embarrassed) Very well . . . only first bring me my little shawl . . . There by the cupboard . . . It's a bit damp here . . .

EPIKHODOV

Very well, miss . . . I'll bring it . . . Now I know what to do with my revolver . . . *(Takes his guitar and exits, strumming)*

YASHA

Two-and-twenty Catastrophes! A stupid man, just between us. *(Yawns)*

DUNYASHA

God forbid he shoots himself.

Pause.

I've become anxious, I worry all the time. I was still a little girl when I was taken into the masters' household, I'm unused to the simple life now, and look how white my hands are, like a young lady's. I've become so pampered, so delicate and genteel, I'm afraid of everything . . . It's scary. And if you deceive me, Yasha, I don't know what will happen to my nerves.

YASHA

(Kisses her) Cute little cucumber! Of course, every girl should remember herself, and what I dislike most of all is a girl who misbehaves.

DUNYASHA

I've fallen passionately in love with you. You're cultivated. You can discuss everything.

Pause.

YASHA

(Yawns) Right, miss ... My opinion is this: if a girl loves somebody, it means she's immoral.

Pause.

It's nice to smoke a cigar in the open air ... *(Listens)* Somebody's coming ... It's the masters ...

Dunyasha embraces him impulsively.

Go home, as if you'd been for a swim in the river, take this path, or else they'll meet you and think we were here together. I couldn't stand that.

DUNYASHA

(Coughs softly) That cigar has given me a headache ... *(Exits)*

Yasha stays, sits by the chapel. Lyubov Andreevna, Gaev and Lopakhin enter.

LOPAKHIN

You've got to decide once and for all—time is running out. The question is quite simple. Do you agree to lease the land for the construction of summer houses or do you not? Answer in one word: yes or no? Just one word!

LYUBOV ANDREEVNA

Who's been smoking disgusting cigars here ... *(Sits down)*

GAEV

They've built the railroad, and it's become convenient. *(Sits down)* Rode to town and had lunch ... yellow into the side! I'd like to go home first and play one game ...

LYUBOV ANDREEVNA

There's no rush.

LOPAKHIN

Just one word! *(Pleadingly)* Give me an answer!

GAEV

(Yawning) Whoso?

LYUBOV ANDREEVNA

(Looking into her purse) Yesterday there was a lot of money, and today there's so little. My poor Varya saves by feeding everybody milk soup, in the kitchen the old folks get nothing but peas, and I waste money somehow senselessly . . . *(She drops her purse, gold coins spill out)* Go on, scatter . . . *(She is annoyed)*

YASHA

Allow me, I'll pick them up at once. *(Collects the coins)*

LYUBOV ANDREEVNA

Be so kind, Yasha. And why did I go to this lunch . . . Your trashy restaurant with its music, with its tablecloths stinking of soap . . . Why drink so much, Lyonya? Why eat so much? Why talk so much? Today in the restaurant you talked too much again, and all beside the point. About the seventies, about the decadents. And to whom? Talking to the waiters about the decadents!

LOPAKHIN

Hm, yes.

GAEV

(Waves his hand) I'm incorrigible, that's obvious . . . *(Vexedly, to Yasha)* Why are you constantly popping up in front of me . . .

YASHA

(Laughing) Just hearing your voice makes me laugh.

GAEV

(To his sister) It's either me, or him . . .

LYUBOV ANDREEVNA

Away with you, Yasha. Go, go . . .

YASHA

(Hands Lyubov Andreevna the purse) I'm leaving. *(Barely restraining his laughter)* Right now . . . *(Exits)*

LOPAKHIN

Rich man Deriganov intends to buy your estate. They say he'll come to the auction in person.

LYUBOV ANDREEVNA

Where did you hear that?

LOPAKHIN

There was talk in town.

GAEV

Our aunt in Yaroslavl has promised to send something, but when and how much nobody knows . . .

LOPAKHIN

How much will she send? A hundred thousand? Two hundred?

LYUBOV ANDREEVNA

Well . . . ten thousand—maybe fifteen, and be thankful for that.

LOPAKHIN

Forgive me, but I have never met such scatterbrained people, such strange, unbusinesslike people, as you two, my friends. I tell you in plain Russian that your estate is going to be sold, and it's as if you don't understand.

LYUBOV ANDREEVNA

What are we to do? Teach us what to do.

LOPAKHIN

I "teach" you every day. Every day I tell you one and the same thing. The cherry orchard and the land have got to be leased out for summer houses. It has got to be done now, as soon as possible—the auction is almost upon us! Understand that! Once you finally decide to have summer houses, you'll get as much money as you like, and then you're saved.

LYUBOV ANDREEVNA

Summer houses, summer people—forgive me, but it's all so banal.

GAEV

I agree with you completely.

LOPAKHIN

I'm going to weep, or scream, or fall down in a faint! I can't stand it! You've worn me out! *(To Gaev)* You old woman!

GAEV

Whoso?

LOPAKHIN

Old woman! *(Starts to leave)*

LYUBOV ANDREEVNA

(Frightened) No, don't leave, stay with us, dear heart! I beg you. Maybe we'll think of something!

LOPAKHIN

What's there to think about?!

LYUBOV ANDREEVNA

Don't leave, I beg you. It's more cheerful, anyhow, with you here ...

Pause.

I keep expecting something, as if the house is going to fall down on us.

GAEV

(Deep in thought) Double into the corner ... *Croisé* into the side ...

LYUBOV ANDREEVNA

We've sinned so very much ...

LOPAKHIN

What kind of sins do you have ...

GAEV

(Puts a fruit drop into his mouth) They say I ate up my whole fortune in fruit drops ... *(Laughs)*

LYUBOV ANDREEVNA

Oh, my sins ... I've always squandered money without stint, like a madwoman, and I married a man who did nothing but run up debts. My husband died from champagne—he drank terribly—and to my misfortune I fell in love with another man, took up with him, and just then—this was my first punishment, a blow right on the head—here, in this river ... my boy drowned, and I went abroad, for good, meaning never to return, never to see this river ... I shut my eyes, I fled, forgetting myself, and *he* followed after me ... mercilessly, crudely. I bought a house near Menton, because he fell ill there, and for three years I got no rest day or night; the sick man wore me out, my soul dried up. And last year, once the house was sold for debts, I left for Paris, and there he fleeced me, abandoned me, took up with another woman, I tried to poison myself ... So stupid, so shameful ... And I suddenly felt drawn back to Russia, to my native land, to my little girl ... *(Wipes her tears)* Lord, Lord, have mercy, forgive me my sins! Don't punish me anymore! *(Takes a telegram from her pocket)* This came today from Paris ... He asks my forgiveness, begs me to come back. *(Tears up the telegram)* Sounds like music somewhere. *(Listens)*

GAEV

It's our famous Jewish band. Remember? Four fiddles, a flute and a double bass.

LYUBOV ANDREEVNA

It still exists? We should get them to come here sometime, arrange an evening.

LOPAKHIN

(Listens) I don't hear anything . . . *(Hums softly)* "The Germans for some ready cash / will frenchify a Russky." *(Laughs)* What a play I saw last night in the theater—very funny.

LYUBOV ANDREEVNA

And most likely it wasn't funny at all. You shouldn't be looking at plays, you should take a look at yourselves. Your life is so gray, you say so much that's unnecessary.

LOPAKHIN

That's true. Let's come right out with it: our life is stupid . . .

Pause.

My father was a peasant, an imbecile, he understood nothing, he taught me nothing, he just got drunk and beat me, and always with a stick. And essentially I'm the same sort of blockhead and imbecile. Never studied anything, my handwriting's vile, I'm ashamed to show people, like a pig's.

LYUBOV ANDREEVNA

You ought to get married, my friend.

LOPAKHIN

Yes . . . That's true.

LYUBOV ANDREEVNA

Maybe to our Varya. She's a nice girl.

LOPAKHIN

Hm, yes.

LYUBOV ANDREEVNA

I took her from simple folk, she works all day, and the main thing is she loves you. And you've liked her since way back.

LOPAKHIN

Well, so? I'm willing . . . She's a nice girl.

Pause.

GAEV

I've been offered a position in the bank. Six thousand a year . . . Have you heard?

LYUBOV ANDREEVNA

Who, you? What an idea . . .

Firs enters bringing a coat.

FIRS

(To Gaev) Please put this on, sir, it's damp.

GAEV

(Puts on coat) I'm sick of you, brother.

FIRS

Ah, well . . . You left this morning without telling me. *(Looks him over)*

LYUBOV ANDREEVNA

How you've aged, Firs!

FIRS

If you please, ma'am.

LOPAKHIN

She says you've aged a lot!

FIRS

I've lived a long time. They were trying to get me married before your father came into the world . . . *(Laughs)* When we got our freedom, I was already head valet. I didn't accept freedom then, I stayed with my masters . . .

Pause.

I remember everybody was glad, but what they were glad about they didn't know themselves.

LOPAKHIN

It was very nice in the old days. At least they had flogging.

FIRS

(Not hearing well) Sure enough. Peasants with the masters, masters with the peasants, but now it's all gone to pieces, you can't figure anything out.

GAEV

Quiet, Firs. I have to go to town tomorrow. They've promised to introduce me to a certain general who can lend me money on credit.

LOPAKHIN

Nothing will come of it. And you won't pay the interest, don't worry.

LYUBOV ANDREEVNA

He's raving. There aren't any generals.

Trofimov, Anya and Varya enter.

GAEV

Look who's coming.

ANYA

Mama's sitting there.

LYUBOV ANDREEVNA

(Tenderly) Come here, come here . . . My darlings . . . *(Embraces Anya and Varya)* If you both only knew how I love you. Sit beside me, here.

They all sit down.

LOPAKHIN

Our eternal student still goes around with young ladies.

TROFIMOV

That's none of your business.

LOPAKHIN

He'll be fifty soon, and he's still a student.

TROFIMOV

Quit your stupid jokes.

LOPAKHIN

Why're you getting angry, you odd duck?

TROFIMOV

Just stop badgering me.

LOPAKHIN

(Laughs) What do you think of me, if I may ask?

TROFIMOV

What I think is this, Ermolai Alexeich: you're a rich man, you'll soon be a millionaire. As there is a need in the food chain for predators who devour everything in their path, so there's a need for you.

Everybody laughs.

VARYA

Petya, why don't you tell us about planets.

LYUBOV ANDREEVNA

No, let's go on with yesterday's conversation.

TROFIMOV

What was it about?

GAEV

The proud man.

TROFIMOV

We talked for a long time yesterday, but didn't come to any conclusion. According to you, there is something mystical in the proud man. Maybe, in your own way, you're right, but if we talk simply, without frills, what is there to be proud of? Does it even make any sense, when man's physiological constitution is none too good, when the vast majority of men are coarse, ignorant and profoundly unhappy? We must stop admiring ourselves. We must work.

GAEV

You die anyway.

TROFIMOV

Who knows? And what does it mean—to die? Maybe man has a hundred senses and death only kills off the five known to us, while the remaining ninety-five remain alive.

LYUBOV ANDREEVNA

You're so intelligent, Petya!

LOPAKHIN

(Ironically) Terribly!

TROFIMOV

The human race goes forward, perfecting its powers. One day all that's beyond its reach now will become close, clear, but we must work, we must give all our strength to helping those who seek the truth. Here in Russia, very few are doing this work right now. The vast majority of the intellectuals I know seek nothing, do nothing, and at the moment are unfit for work. They call themselves intellectuals, but they talk down to servants, treat peasants like animals, study poorly, read nothing serious, do precisely nothing, their science is only talk, and they have little understanding of art. They're all serious, they all have solemn faces, they all talk only about important things, they philosophize, and meanwhile, in front of their eyes, workers eat disgusting food, sleep without pillows, thirty or forty to a room, with bedbugs everywhere, stench, dankness, moral filth . . . And all the nice talk is obviously aimed at distracting attention, our own and other people's. Show me where those day nurseries are that are talked about so much and so often? Where are the reading rooms? They're only written about in novels; in reality there aren't any. There's only dirt, banality, barbarism . . . Serious faces scare me; I don't like them. Serious conversations scare me. Better to be quiet!

LOPAKHIN

You know, I get up at five in the morning, work from morning till night, and I'm constantly dealing with money, my own and other people's, so I see what sort of people are around. You only need to start doing something, to realize how few honest, decent people there are. Sometimes, when I can't fall asleep, I think: "Lord, you gave us vast forests, boundless fields, the deepest horizons, and we who live here should be real giants ourselves . . ."

LYUBOV ANDREEVNA

What do you need giants for . . . They're only good in fairy tales, otherwise they're frightening.

Epikhodov passes by upstage playing the guitar.

(Pensively) There goes Epikhodov . . .

ANYA

(Pensively) There goes Epikhodov . . .

GAEV

The sun has set, ladies and gentlemen.

TROFIMOV

Yes.

GAEV

(In a low voice, as if declaiming) O nature, wondrous nature, you shine with eternal radiance, beautiful and indifferent, you, whom we call mother, in yourself you combine being and death, you give life and you destroy . . .

VARYA

(Pleadingly) Uncle dear!

ANYA

You're at it again, uncle!

TROFIMOV

Better double the yellow into the side.

GAEV

I'll be quiet, I'll be quiet.

They all sit deep in thought. Silence. Only Firs's quiet muttering can be heard. Suddenly there is a distant sound, as if from the sky, the sound of a breaking string, dying away, sad.

LYUBOV ANDREEVNA

What was that?

LOPAKHIN

I don't know. Somewhere far away in a mine a bucket chain snapped. But somewhere very far away.

GAEV

Maybe it was some bird . . . like a heron.

TROFIMOV

Or a barn owl . . .

LYUBOV ANDREEVNA

(Shudders) It's unpleasant somehow.

Pause.

FIRS

It was the same before the catastrophe: the owl screeched, and the samovar went on whistling.

GAEV

Before what catastrophe?

FIRS

Freedom.

Pause.

LYUBOV ANDREEVNA

You know what, my friends, let's go, it's already evening. *(To Anya)* You have tears in your eyes . . . What is it, my girl? *(Embraces her)*

ANYA

I just do, mama. It's nothing.

TROFIMOV

Somebody's coming.

A passerby appears in a shabby white cap and an overcoat, slightly drunk.

PASSERBY

May I ask if I can go straight to the station from here?

GAEV

You can. Just down this road.

PASSERBY

Much obliged to you. *(Coughs)* Splendid weather . . . *(Declaims)*
Brother, my suffering brother . . . come down to the Volga. Whose
moaning . . . *(To Varya)* Mademoiselle, might a starving Russian
have thirty kopecks . . .

Varya cries out in fear.

LOPAKHIN

(Angrily, to himself) For every outrage, there is decency!

LYUBOV ANDREEVNA

(Nonplussed) Here . . . Take this . . . *(Rummages in her purse)* No
silver . . . Never mind, here's a gold piece for you . . .

PASSERBY

Much obliged to you! *(Exits)*

Laughter.

VARYA

(Frightened) I'm leaving . . . I'm leaving . . . Oh, mama, the people
at home have nothing to eat, and you gave him a gold piece.

LYUBOV ANDREEVNA

What can you do with a fool like me?! At home I'll give you all
I have. Ermolai Alexeich, lend me some more! . . .

LOPAKHIN

Yes, ma'am.

LYUBOV ANDREEVNA

Let's go, ladies and gentlemen, it's time. And we've just made you
a match here, Varya. Congratulations.

VARYA

(Through tears) You shouldn't joke about that, mama.

LOPAKHIN

Ofoolia, get thee to a nunnery . . .

GAEV

My hands are shaking: I haven't played billiards for so long.

LOPAKHIN

Ofoolia, O nymph, remember me in thy orisons!

LYUBOV ANDREEVNA

Let's go, ladies and gentlemen. It's nearly suppertime.

VARYA

He frightened me. My heart's pounding.

LOPAKHIN

I remind you, ladies and gentlemen: on August twenty-second the cherry orchard will go up for sale. Think about it! . . . Think! . . .

Exit all but Trofimov and Anya.

ANYA

(Laughing) Thanks to that man who frightened Varya, we're alone now.

TROFIMOV

Varya's afraid we'll up and fall in love with each other, so she clings to us all day. With her narrow mind, she can't understand that we're higher than love. To go beyond the petty and illusory that keep us from being free and happy—that is the goal and meaning of our life. Forward! We go irrepressibly towards the bright star that shines there in the distance! Forward! Don't lag behind, my friends!

ANYA

(Clasping her hands) How well you speak!

Pause.

It's wonderful here today!

TROFIMOV

Yes, the weather is astonishing.

ANYA

What have you done to me, Petya? Why don't I love the cherry orchard the way I used to? I loved it so dearly, I thought there was no better place on earth than our orchard.

TROFIMOV

All Russia is our orchard. The earth is vast and beautiful, there are many marvelous places on it.

Pause.

Think, Anya: your grandfather, your great-grandfather, and all your ancestors were serf-owners, owners of human souls. Can it be that human beings don't look at you from every cherry, from every leaf, from every tree trunk of this orchard, that you don't hear their voices? . . . To own living souls—it transformed you all, those who lived before and those living now, so that your mother, you, your uncle no longer notice that you are living on credit, at the expense of others, at the expense of people you won't allow across your threshold . . . We're at least two hundred years behind, we still have precisely nothing, no definite attitude towards the past. We only philosophize, complain of our anguish, or drink vodka. Yet it's so clear that to begin to live in the present, we must first atone for our past, be done with it, and we can only atone for it through suffering, only through extraordinary, relentless labor. Understand that, Anya.

ANYA

For a long time now the house we live in hasn't been ours, and I shall leave, I give you my word.

TROFIMOV

If you have the keys of the household, throw them down the well and walk away. Be free as the wind.

ANYA

(Ecstatically) How well you put it!

TROFIMOV

Believe me, Anya, believe me! I'm not thirty yet, I'm young, I'm still a student, but I've already been through so much! Winter comes, I'm hungry, sick, anxious, poor as a beggar, and—is there anywhere fate hasn't driven me, is there anywhere I haven't been?! And yet always, every moment, day and night, my soul is filled with inexplicable premonitions. I have a premonition of happiness, Anya, I see it already . . .

ANYA

(Pensively) The moon is rising.

The sound of Epikhodov's guitar is heard, playing the same melancholy song.

The moon rises. Somewhere near the poplars Varya is looking for Anya and calling: "Anya! Where are you?"

TROFIMOV

Yes, the moon is rising.

Pause.

Here it is, happiness, here it comes, getting closer and closer, I can already hear its footsteps. And if we don't see it, if we don't come to know it—so what? Others will!

Voice of Varya: "Anya! Where are you?"

That Varya again! *(Angrily)* Outrageous!

ANYA

Well, then, let's go to the river. It's nice there.

TROFIMOV

Let's go.

They exit.
  Varya's voice: "Anya! Anya!"
  Curtain.

ACT THREE

The drawing room, separated by an archway from the ballroom. The chandelier is lit. A Jewish band, the same one mentioned in the second act, is playing in the front hall.

Evening. People in the ballroom are dancing a grand-rond. The voice of Simeonov-Pishchik: "Promenade à une paire!" Dancing couples come out into the drawing room: first Pishchik and Charlotta, then Trofimov and Lyubov Andreevna, then Anya and the postal clerk, then Varya and the stationmaster, and so on. Varya quietly weeps and wipes her tears as she dances. Dunyasha is in the last couple. They go back into the ballroom. Pishchik calls out: "Grand-rond, balancez!" and "Les cavaliers à genoux et remerciez vos dames!"

Firs, dressed in a tailcoat, serves seltzer water on a tray. Pishchik and Trofimov enter the drawing room.

PISHCHIK

My heart's pumping, I've already had two strokes, it's hard for me to dance, but, as they say, when you run with the pack, there's no turning back. Still, I'm healthy as a horse. My late father, may he

153

rest in peace, liked to joke. He used to say that our ancient family of the Simeonov-Pishchiks goes back to that very same horse
Caligula gave a seat to in the Senate . . . *(Sits down)* But the trouble
is: no money! A hungry dog believes only in meat . . . *(Snores and
wakes up at once)* Same with me . . . only it's money . . .

TROFIMOV

In fact, you do have a certain horsey look.

PISHCHIK

Well, so . . . the horse is a good beast . . . you can sell a horse . . .

*The sound of billiards comes from the next room. Varya appears
under the archway of the ballroom.*

TROFIMOV

(Teasing) Madame Lopakhin! Madame Lopakhin! . . .

VARYA

(Angrily) Mangy mister!

TROFIMOV

Yes, I'm a mangy mister, and proud of it!

VARYA

(Pondering bitterly) We've hired musicians, and how are we going
to pay them? *(Exits)*

TROFIMOV

(To Pishchik) If you had found some other use for all the energy
you've spent in the course of your life scraping up the money to
pay your interest, you might have stood the world on its head.

PISHCHIK

Nietzsche . . . a philosopher . . . the greatest, the most famous . . . a
man of vast intelligence, says in his writings that it's permitted to
make counterfeit money.

TROFIMOV

So you've read Nietzsche?

PISHCHIK

Well . . . Dashenka told me. And I'm in such a position now that I might as well go and start counterfeiting . . . In two days I have to pay back three hundred and ten roubles . . . I've already got hold of a hundred and thirty . . . *(Feels anxiously in his pockets)* The money's vanished! I've lost the money! *(Through tears)* Where's the money? *(Joyfully)* Ah, here it is, in the lining . . . I even broke into a sweat . . .

Lyubov Andreevna and Charlotta Ivanovna enter.

LYUBOV ANDREEVNA

(Humming a lively Georgian dance tune) Why is Leonid taking so long? What's he doing in town? *(To Dunyasha)* Dunyasha, offer the musicians some tea . . .

TROFIMOV

The auction probably didn't take place.

LYUBOV ANDREEVNA

It was the wrong time for musicians, the wrong time for a ball . . . Well, never mind . . . *(Sits down and hums softly)*

CHARLOTTA

(Hands Pishchik a deck of cards) Here's a deck of cards, think of a card, any card.

PISHCHIK

Ready.

CHARLOTTA

Now shuffle the deck. Very good. Now give it to me, my dear Mr. Pishchik. *Eins, zwei, drei!* Now look in your side pocket, it's there . . .

PISHCHIK

(Takes a card from his side pocket) The eight of spades, absolutely right! *(Surprised)* Imagine that!

CHARLOTTA

(Holds the deck out on her palm to Trofimov) Tell me quickly, which card is on top?

TROFIMOV

Oh, let's say the queen of spades.

CHARLOTTA

Right! *(To Pishchik)* Well, which card is on top?

PISHCHIK

The ace of hearts.

CHARLOTTA

Right! *(Slaps her palm, the deck of cards disappears)* What nice weather today!

A mysterious woman's voice answers her as if from underground: "Oh, yes, magnificent weather, my lady."

You're so nice, my ideal man . . .

The voice: "I am also liking you very much, my lady."

STATIONMASTER

(Applauds) Bravo, madam ventriloquist!

PISHCHIK

(Surprised) Imagine that! Most charming Charlotta Ivanovna . . . I'm simply in love with you . . .

CHARLOTTA

In love? *(Shrugging)* So you're able to love? *Guter Mensch, aber schlechter Musikant.*

TROFIMOV

(Slaps Pishchik on the shoulder) There's a good horse . . .

CHARLOTTA

Attention please, one more trick. *(Takes a blanket from a chair)* Here's a very fine blanket, I have the wish to sell it . . . *(Holds it up)* Does anyone wish to buy it?

PISHCHIK

(Surprised) Imagine that!

CHARLOTTA

Eins, zwei, drei!

She quickly moves the blanket aside; behind it stands Anya. She curtsies, runs to her mother, embraces her, and runs back to the ballroom amidst general delight.

LYUBOV ANDREEVNA

(Applauds) Bravo, bravo! . . .

CHARLOTTA

Once more now! *Eins, zwei, drei!*

She moves the blanket aside; Varya is standing behind it and bows.

PISHCHIK

(Surprised) Imagine that!

CHARLOTTA

The end! *(Throws the blanket over Pishchik, curtseys, and runs off to the ballroom)*

PISHCHIK

(Hurries after her) Wicked woman . . . isn't she? Isn't she? *(Exits)*

LYUBOV ANDREEVNA

And still no Leonid. What he's doing so long in town, I don't understand. Everything must be finished there, the estate has been sold, or the auction didn't take place. Why keep me in the dark for so long?!

VARYA

(Trying to comfort her) Uncle has bought it, I'm sure of that.

TROFIMOV

(Mockingly) Oh, yes.

VARYA

Our great-aunt sent him the power of attorney to buy it in her name with the transfer of the debt. She did it for Anya. And I'm sure, with God's help, uncle will buy it.

LYUBOV ANDREEVNA

Your great-aunt from Yaroslavl sent fifteen thousand to buy the estate in *her* name—she doesn't trust us—and that money isn't even enough to pay the interest. *(Covers her face with her hands)* Today my fate is being decided, my fate . . .

TROFIMOV

(Teases Varya) Madame Lopakhin!

VARYA

(Angrily) Eternal student! Already expelled twice from the university.

LYUBOV ANDREEVNA

Why do you get angry, Varya? He teases you about Lopakhin—what of it? Marry Lopakhin, if you want to. He's a good, interesting man. If you don't want to—don't. Nobody's forcing you, my sweet . . .

VARYA

For me it's a very serious matter, mama, to be honest. He's a good man, I like him.

LYUBOV ANDREEVNA

So marry him. I don't understand what you're waiting for!

VARYA

But, mama, I can't propose to him myself. For two years now everybody's been talking to me about him. Everybody talks, but he either says nothing or makes jokes. I understand. He's getting rich, he's busy, he can't be bothered with me. If only I had some money, just a little, just a hundred roubles, I'd drop everything, I'd go far, far away. I'd go to a convent.

TROFIMOV

What blessedness!

VARYA

(To Trofimov) Students are supposed to be intelligent! *(In a soft voice, through tears)* How unattractive you've become, Petya, how you've aged! *(To Lyubov Andreevna, no longer tearful)* Only I can't just sit idle, mama. I have to be doing something every minute.

Yasha enters.

YASHA

(Barely able to keep from laughing) Epikhodov just broke a billiard cue! . . . *(Exits)*

VARYA

What is Epikhodov doing here? Who allowed him to play billiards? I don't understand these people . . . *(Exits)*

LYUBOV ANDREEVNA

Don't tease her, Petya. You can see she's unhappy as it is.

TROFIMOV

She's so officious, always poking her nose into other people's business. She hasn't left Anya and me alone all summer, for fear we might start a romance. What business is it of hers? Besides, I never gave any sign of it, I'm far from such banality. We're higher than love!

LYUBOV ANDREEVNA

Then I must be lower than love. *(In great anxiety)* Why isn't Leonid here? If only I knew whether the estate's been sold or not! This catastrophe seems so incredible to me, I somehow don't even know what to think, I'm at a loss . . . I could scream . . . I could do something stupid. Save me, Petya. Say something, go on, say something . . .

TROFIMOV

Does it make any difference whether the estate gets sold today or not? It was all finished long ago, there's no turning back, the path is overgrown. Calm down, my dear. Don't deceive yourself. You must face the truth at least once in your life.

LYUBOV ANDREEVNA

What truth? You can see where truth is and where it isn't, but I seem to have lost my sight, I don't see anything. You boldly resolve all the important questions, but tell me, darling, isn't that because you're young, because you haven't had time to suffer for a single one of your questions? You boldly look ahead, but isn't that because you don't see or expect anything terrible, because life is still concealed from your young eyes? You're bolder, deeper, more honest than we are, but think about it, show just a fingertip of generosity, have mercy on me. I was born here, my father and mother lived here, and my grandfather, I love this house, I can't conceive of my life without the cherry orchard, and if it's so necessary to sell it, then sell me along with it . . . *(Embraces Trofimov, kisses him on the forehead)* My son drowned here . . . *(Weeps)* You're a good, kind man: have pity on me.

TROFIMOV

You know I sympathize with all my heart.

LYUBOV ANDREEVNA

Yes, but couldn't you ... couldn't you say it some other way? ...
(Takes out a handkerchief, a telegram falls on the floor) My soul is
weighed down today, you can't imagine. It's noisy for me here, my
soul trembles at every sound, I tremble all over, but I can't go to my
room, I'm afraid to be alone in the silence. Don't judge me, Petya ...
I love you like one of my own. I'd gladly have you marry Anya,
I swear I would, only you must study, darling, you must finish your
education. You don't do anything, fate just tosses you from one
place to another, it's so strange ... Isn't it? And you should do
something about your beard, make it grow somehow ... *(Laughs)*
You're so funny!

TROFIMOV

(Picks up the telegram) I have no wish to be handsome.

LYUBOV ANDREEVNA

It's a telegram from Paris. I get one every day. One yesterday, one
today. This savage man is sick again, things are going badly again ...
He asks my forgiveness, begs me to come back, and I really ought
to go to Paris and be with him. You're making a stern face, Petya,
but what am I to do, darling, what am I to do, he's ill, he's lonely,
unhappy, and who will look after him, who will keep him from
making mistakes, who will give him his medicine on time? And
why hide it or keep silent? I love him, it's obvious. I love him, I love
him ... He's a millstone around my neck, he's dragging me down
with him, but I love this stone and can't live without it. *(She presses
Trofimov's hand)* Don't think ill of me, Petya, don't say anything to
me, don't ...

TROFIMOV

(Through tears) Forgive my frankness, but, for God's sake, the man
fleeced you!

LYUBOV ANDREEVNA

No, no, no, you mustn't speak that way ... *(Covers her ears)*

TROFIMOV

He's a scoundrel, you're the only one who doesn't know it! He's a petty scoundrel, a nothing . . .

LYUBOV ANDREEVNA

(Angrily, but restraining herself) You're twenty-six or twenty-seven years old, but you're still a schoolboy!

TROFIMOV

So what if I am!

LYUBOV ANDREEVNA

You should be a man, at your age you should understand what it is to love. And you yourself should love . . . you should fall in love! *(Angrily)* Yes, yes! You're not all that pure, you're just a squeamish, silly, eccentric little freak . . .

TROFIMOV

(Horrified) What is she saying!

LYUBOV ANDREEVNA

"I'm higher than love!" You're not higher than love, you're simply, as our Firs here says, a blunderhead. Not to have a mistress at your age! . . .

TROFIMOV

(Horrified) This is terrible! What is she saying?! *(Goes quickly toward the ballroom, clutching his head)* This is terrible . . . I can't stand it, I'm leaving . . . *(Goes out, but comes back at once)* It's all over between us! *(Exits to the front hall)*

LYUBOV ANDREEVNA

(Shouts after him) Petya, wait! Silly man, I was joking! Petya!

The sound of someone's quick steps on the stairs, then a sudden crash. Anya and Varya cry out, but at once laughter is heard.

What was that?

Anya runs in.

ANYA

(Laughing) Petya fell down the stairs! *(Runs out)*

LYUBOV ANDREEVNA

What a funny one this Petya is ... *(Follows her out)*

The stationmaster stands in the middle of the ballroom and recites "The Sinful Woman," by A. K. Tolstoy:

STATIONMASTER

Mirth and laughter from the crowd,
Lutes and cymbals ringing loud,
Flowers and garlands all around,
Brocade curtains hanging down,
Brightly trimmed with gleaming braid,
Palace halls richly arrayed,
Gold and crystal everywhere ...

They all listen, but after he has read a few lines, the sounds of a waltz come from the front hall and the reading breaks off. They all dance. Trofimov, Anya, Varya and Lyubov Andreevna come from the front hall.

LYUBOV ANDREEVNA

Well, Petya ... you pure soul ... I ask your forgiveness ... Let's dance ... *(Dances with Petya)*

Anya and Varya dance. Firs enters, places his stick by the side door. Yasha also enters and watches the dancing.

YASHA

What is it, grandpa?

FIRS

Not feeling well. In the old days we had generals, barons and admirals dancing at our balls, and now we send for the postal clerk and the stationmaster, and even they aren't so eager to come. I've grown a bit weak. My late master, the grandfather, treated everybody with sealing wax, for all ailments. I've been taking sealing wax every day for twenty years, if not more; maybe that's why I'm still alive.

YASHA

I'm sick of you, grandpa. *(Yawns)* Why don't you just up and croak . . .

FIRS

Eh, you . . . blunderhead! *(Mutters)*

Trofimov and Lyubov Andreevna dance in the ballroom, then in the drawing room.

LYUBOV ANDREEVNA

Merci. I'll sit for a while . . . *(Sits down)* I'm tired.

Anya enters.

ANYA

(Excited) A man in the kitchen said just now that the cherry orchard was sold today.

LYUBOV ANDREEVNA

Sold to whom?

ANYA

He didn't say. He left. *(Dances with Trofimov, both exit to the ballroom)*

YASHA

It was some old man there babbling. A stranger.

FIRS

And Leonid Andreich still isn't here, he hasn't come. He's wearing a light coat, demi-season, he's likely to catch cold. Ehh, green youth!

LYUBOV ANDREEVNA

I'm going to die right here and now. Go, Yasha, find out who bought it.

YASHA

But the old man's long gone. *(Laughs)*

LYUBOV ANDREEVNA

(Slightly annoyed) Well, what are you laughing at? What are you glad about?

YASHA

Epikhodov's so funny. A worthless man. Two-and-twenty Catastrophes.

LYUBOV ANDREEVNA

If the estate is sold, Firs, where will you go?

FIRS

Wherever you tell me.

LYUBOV ANDREEVNA

Why such a face? Are you unwell? You know, you should go to bed ...

FIRS

Oh, yes ... *(With a grin)* I'll go to bed, and who will serve here without me, who'll be in charge? I'm the only one in the whole house.

YASHA

(To Lyubov Andreevna) Lyubov Andreevna! Please allow me to address you with a request. If you go back to Paris, do me the favor of taking me with you. It is absolutely impossible for me to remain here. *(Looking around, in a low voice)* What's there to talk about, you can see for yourself it's an uneducated country, the people are immoral, and besides it's boring, they feed us execrably in the

kitchen, and then there's this Firs going around muttering all sorts of inanities. Please take me with you!

Pishchik enters.

PISHCHIK

Allow me to invite you . . . for a little waltz, most excellent lady . . . *(Lyubov Andreevna gets up and dances with him)* Charming lady, I'll still get a hundred and eighty little roubles from you . . . I will . . . *(Dances)* A hundred and eighty little roubles . . .

They pass into the ballroom.

YASHA

(Humming softly) "Oh, wilt thou grasp the stirrings of my soul . . ."

In the ballroom, a figure in a gray top hat and checkered trousers leaps and waves its arms; there are shouts of: "Bravo, Charlotta Ivanovna!"

DUNYASHA

(Stops to powder her nose) The young miss told me to dance—there are lots of gentlemen, and not enough ladies—and I get dizzy from dancing, my heart is pounding, Firs Nikolaevich, and the postal clerk just said something to me that took my breath away.

The music dies down.

FIRS

What did he say to you?

DUNYASHA

You, he said, are like a flower.

YASHA

(Yawns) Ignorance . . . *(Exits)*

DUNYASHA

Like a flower. I'm such a delicate girl, I'm terribly fond of tender words.

FIRS

You'll take a tumble.

Epikhodov enters.

EPIKHODOV

So you don't want to see me, Avdotya Fyodorovna . . . as if I'm some sort of insect. *(Sighs)* Life!

DUNYASHA

What can I do for you?

EPIKHODOV

Doubtless, you may be right. *(Sighs)* But if you look at it from the point of view, then, if I may put it so, forgive my frankness, you absolutely drove me into a state of mind. I know my fortune, every day some sort of catastrophe befalls me, and to that I have long been accustomed, so that I look upon my fate with a smile. You gave me your word, and though I . . .

DUNYASHA

Let's talk about it later, I beg you, and now leave me alone. Right now I'm dreaming. *(Plays with her fan)*

EPIKHODOV

Catastrophes happen to me every day, and, if I may put it so, I only smile, even laugh.

Varya enters from the ballroom.

VARYA

You still haven't left, Semyon? Really, how can you be so disrespectful! *(To Dunyasha)* Go, Dunyasha. *(To Epikhodov)* First you play billiards and break a cue, then you strut around the drawing room as if you're a guest.

EPIKHODOV

You can't exact anything from me, if I may put it so.

VARYA

I'm not "exacting" anything from you, I'm telling you. All you do is wander around from place to place, and you don't do any work. We keep a clerk, but who knows why.

EPIKHODOV

(Offended) Whether I work, or wander, or eat, or play billiards—that can be discussed only by mature and understanding people.

VARYA

How dare you say that to me! *(Flaring up)* How dare you! So I don't understand anything? Get out of here! This minute!

EPIKHODOV

(Turning coward) I ask you to express yourself in a more delicate manner.

VARYA

(Beside herself) Get out of here, this very minute! Out!

He goes toward the door; she follows him.

Two-and-twenty Catastrophes! Don't you set foot in here again. Don't let me lay eyes on you!

Epikhodov exits; his voice comes from outside the door: "I shall lodge a complaint against you."

Ah, so you're coming back? *(Grabs the stick Firs has left by the door)* Come on, then . . . come on . . . come on, I'll show you . . . Ah, so you're coming? You're really coming? Take this then . . . *(She swings the stick just as Lopakhin enters)*

LOPAKHIN

My humble thanks.

VARYA

(Angrily and mockingly) Very sorry!

LOPAKHIN

Never mind, miss. I humbly thank you for the pleasant treatment.

VARYA

Don't mention it. *(Steps away, then looks at him and asks softly)* Did I hurt you?

LOPAKHIN

No, it's nothing. It'll give me a hu-u-uge bump, though.

Voices in the ballroom: "Lopakhin's here! Ermolai Alexeich!"

PISHCHIK

Ah, long have we waited, long have we wondered . . . *(Exchanges kisses with Lopakhin)* There's a whiff of cognac coming off you, my dear heart. We're having a good time here, too.

Lyubov Andreevna enters.

LYUBOV ANDREEVNA

It's you, Ermolai Alexeich? What took you so long? Where's Leonid?

LOPAKHIN

Leonid Andreich arrived with me, he's coming . . .

LYUBOV ANDREEVNA

(Nervously) Well, so? Did the auction take place? Tell me!

LOPAKHIN

(Embarrassed, afraid of displaying his joy) The auction was over by four o'clock ... We missed the train, had to wait for the nine-thirty. *(With a heavy sigh)* Oof! I'm still a bit giddy ...

Gaev enters; he is holding his purchases in his right hand and wiping his tears with his left.

LYUBOV ANDREEVNA

Lyonya, what is it? Well, Lyonya? *(Impatiently, with tears)* Quickly, for God's sake ...

GAEV

(Makes no reply, only waves his hand; to Firs, weeping) Here, take them ... There are anchovies, Kerch herring ... I haven't eaten at all today ... What I've been through!

The door to the billiard room is open; the click of billiard balls is heard and Yasha's voice: "Seven and eighteen!" Gaev's expression changes; he no longer weeps.

I'm awfully tired. Bring me a change of clothes, Firs. *(Goes through the ballroom to his own room. Firs follows)*

PISHCHIK

What happened at the auction? Tell us!

LYUBOV ANDREEVNA

Was the cherry orchard sold?

LOPAKHIN

Yes, it was.

LYUBOV ANDREEVNA

Who bought it?

LOPAKHIN

I bought it.

Pause.

Lyubov Andreevna is crushed; she would have fallen if she had not been standing by an armchair and a table. Varya takes the keys from her belt, flings them onto the floor in the middle of the drawing room, and exits.

I bought it! Wait, ladies and gentlemen, please, my head's in a fog, I can't speak . . . *(Laughs)* We came to the auction, Deriganov was already there. Leonid Andreich only had fifteen thousand, and Deriganov immediately bid thirty on top of the debt. I see how it goes, I take him up on it and bid forty. He goes up to forty-five. I go up to fifty-five. He keeps adding five, I keep adding ten . . . Well, in the end I bid ninety on top of the debt, and I got it. The cherry orchard's mine now! Mine! *(Laughs loudly)* Oh, Lord God, the cherry orchard's mine! Tell me I'm drunk, I'm out of my mind, I'm imagining it all . . . *(Stamps his feet)* Don't laugh at me! If only my father and grandfather could rise from their graves and look at this whole thing, at their Ermolai, their beaten, barely literate Ermolai, who ran around barefoot in the winter, at how this same Ermolai bought the estate, than which there's nothing more beautiful in the world. I bought the estate where my grandfather and father were slaves, where they weren't even allowed into the kitchen. I'm dreaming, I'm making it up, it only seems so . . . It's the fruit of your imagination, covered in the darkness of the unknown . . . *(Picks up the keys, smiling tenderly)* She threw down the keys. She wants to show she's no longer in charge here . . . *(Jingles the keys)* Well, it makes no difference.

Sounds of the band tuning up.

Hey, musicians, play, let's hear it! Come on, everybody, watch Ermolai Lopakhin take the axe to the cherry orchard, watch the trees fall down! We'll build summer houses, and our grandchildren and great-grandchildren will see a new life here . . . Music, play!

Music plays. Lyubov Andreevna sinks into a chair and weeps bitterly.

(With reproach) Why, why didn't you listen to me? My poor dear, there's no going back now. *(In tears)* Oh, if only all this could be over quickly, if only our senseless, luckless life could change quickly.

PISHCHIK

(Takes him under the arm, in a half whisper) She's crying. Let's go to the ballroom and leave her alone ... Come on. *(Takes him under the arm and leads him to the ballroom)*

LOPAKHIN

What's going on? Music, louder! Let everything be the way I want it! *(With irony)* Here comes the new landlord, the owner of the cherry orchard! *(Accidentally shoves a little table, almost tips over the candelabra)* I can pay for everything! *(Exits with Pishchik)*

There is no one in the ballroom and the drawing room except Lyubov Andreevna, who sits huddled up and weeps bitterly. Music plays softly. Anya and Trofimov enter quickly. Anya goes to her mother and kneels before her. Trofimov remains by the entrance to the ballroom.

ANYA

Mama! ... Mama, you're crying? My dear, kind, good mama, my beautiful mama, I love you ... I bless you. The cherry orchard's been sold, it's no more, that's true, that's true, but don't cry, mama, you still have your life ahead of you, you still have your good, pure soul ... Come with me, come, dearest, let's go away from here, come! ... We'll plant a new orchard, more luxuriant than this one, you'll see it, you'll understand, and joy, a quiet, deep joy, will descend into your soul, like the sun at evening, and you'll smile, mama! Come, my dear! Come! ...

Curtain.

ACT FOUR

The same set as Act One. There are no curtains on the windows, no paintings on the walls; there is some furniture left, piled up in one corner as if for a sale. There is a feeling of emptiness. Suitcases, bundles, and so on are piled up by the exit door and at the back of the stage. The door to the left is open; Varya and Anya's voices come from there. Lopakhin stands waiting. Yasha holds a tray of glasses filled with champagne. In the front hall Epikhodov is tying up a box. Noise comes from deep backstage. It is peasants who have come to say good-bye. Gaev's voice says: "Thank you, brothers, thank you."

YASHA

The simple folk have come to say good-bye. My opinion is this, Ermolai Alexeich: they're good folk, but they understand very little.

The noise dies down. Lyubov Andreevna and Gaev enter through the front hall. She no longer weeps, but she is pale, her face twitches, and she is unable to speak.

173

GAEV

You gave them your purse, Lyuba. Impossible! Impossible!

LYUBOV ANDREEVNA

I couldn't help it! I couldn't help it!

Both exit.

LOPAKHIN

(Through the doorway, calls after them) Wait, I humbly beg you! A little glass for the road. I didn't think to bring it from town, and they only had one bottle at the station. Wait!

Pause.

So, you don't want to? *(Steps away from the door)* If I'd known, I wouldn't have bought it. Well, I won't drink either, then.

Yasha carefully sets the tray on a chair.

Yasha, you drink at least.

YASHA

To those who are leaving! Good luck to those who are staying! *(He drinks)* This is not real champagne, I can assure you.

LOPAKHIN

Eight roubles a bottle.

Pause.

It's damned cold here.

YASHA

Didn't heat it today. We're leaving anyway. *(Laughs)*

LOPAKHIN

What's with you?

YASHA

I'm delighted.

LOPAKHIN

It's October, but sunny and calm, like summer. Good for building. *(Glancing at his watch, says through the door)* Bear in mind, ladies and gentlemen, that the train comes in forty-six minutes! Which means you should leave for the station in twenty minutes. Hurry it up.

Trofimov enters from outside wearing an overcoat.

TROFIMOV

I suppose it's already time to go. They've brought the horses. Devil knows where my galoshes are. Vanished. *(Through the door)* Anya, where are my galoshes? I can't find them!

LOPAKHIN

And I must go to Kharkov. I'm taking the same train as you. I'll spend the whole winter in Kharkov. All this hanging around with you and doing nothing has worn me out. I can't get by without work, I don't know what to do with my hands, they hang there somehow strangely, like somebody else's.

TROFIMOV

We'll be gone soon, and you can go back to your useful labors.

LOPAKHIN

Have a little glass.

TROFIMOV

None for me.

LOPAKHIN

So, it's Moscow now?

TROFIMOV

Yes, I'll see them off in town, and tomorrow it's Moscow.

LOPAKHIN

Yes . . . No doubt the professors are holding off their lectures, waiting for you to come!

TROFIMOV

That's none of your business.

LOPAKHIN

How many years have you been studying at the university?

TROFIMOV

Try thinking up something new. That's old and stale. *(Looking for his galoshes)* You know, we may just never see each other again, so allow me to give you a piece of parting advice: stop waving your arms! Get out of this habit of waving your arms. And building summer houses, calculating that in time the summer people will turn into independent farmers, calculating like that—is also waving your arms . . . Anyhow, I still like you. You have fine, delicate fingers, like an artist; you have a fine, delicate soul . . .

LOPAKHIN

(Embraces him) Good-bye, dear boy. Thanks for everything. Take some money from me for the road, if you need it.

TROFIMOV

Why should I? There's no need.

LOPAKHIN

But you haven't got any!

TROFIMOV

Yes, I have. Thanks very much. I got some for a translation. It's right here in my pocket. *(Anxiously)* But where are my galoshes?!

VARYA

(From the other room) Here, take the vile things! *(Throws a pair of rubber galoshes onto the stage)*

TROFIMOV

What are you angry about, Varya? Hm . . . No, these aren't my galoshes.

LOPAKHIN

I sowed three thousand acres of poppies in the spring, and just made forty thousand. When my poppies flowered, what a picture it was! So, as I say, I made forty thousand, and I'm offering to lend you some, because I can. Why turn up your nose? I'm a peasant . . . let's keep it simple.

TROFIMOV

Your father was a peasant, mine was a druggist, and from that follows—absolutely nothing.

Lopakhin takes out his wallet.

Stop, stop . . . I won't take it, even if it's two hundred thousand. I'm a free man. Nothing that all of you, rich and poor, value so highly and dearly, has the least power over me, any more than this bit of fluff floating in the air. I can get along without you, I can pass you by, I'm strong and proud. Mankind is striding towards the highest truth, towards the highest happiness possible on earth, and I am in the forefront!

LOPAKHIN

Will you get there?

TROFIMOV

I will.

Pause.

I will get there, or I will show others the way.

The sound of an axe striking wood is heard.

LOPAKHIN

Well, good-bye, dear boy. It's time to go. Here we are turning up our noses at each other, and meanwhile life is passing by. When I work for a long time without a break, my thoughts become lighter, and it seems as if I also know why I exist. But there are so many people in Russia, brother, who exist with no idea why. Well, never mind, that's not what keeps things circulating. They say Leonid Andreich has taken a position in the bank, six thousand a year . . . Only he won't keep it, he's too lazy . . .

ANYA

(In the doorway) Mama asks you to wait till she leaves before you cut down the orchard.

TROFIMOV

You might indeed show a bit more tact . . . *(Exits through front hall)*

LOPAKHIN

All right, all right . . . What's with them, really! *(Exits after him)*

ANYA

Has Firs been sent to the hospital?

YASHA

I told them this morning. I suppose it's been done.

ANYA

(To Epikhodov, who passes through the room) Semyon Panteleich, please find out if Firs has been sent to the hospital.

YASHA

(Offended) I told Egor this morning. Why ask ten times!

EPIKHODOV

The long-lived Firs, in my definitive opinion, is not fit for repair. He ought to join his ancestors. And I can only envy him. *(Places a suitcase on a hat box and crushes it)* Well, there, of course. I just knew it. *(Exits)*

YASHA

(Mockingly) Two-and-twenty Catastrophes . . .

VARYA

(Behind the door) Has Firs been taken to the hospital?

ANYA

Yes, he has.

VARYA

Why didn't they take the letter for the doctor?

ANYA

They'll have to send it after him . . . *(Exits)*

VARYA

(From the next room) Where's Yasha? Tell him his mother has come and wants to say good-bye to him.

YASHA

(Waves his hand) I'm at the end of my patience!

Dunyasha has been fussing with the luggage all the while; now that Yasha is left alone, she goes up to him.

DUNYASHA

You might look at me at least once, Yasha. You're leaving . . . you're abandoning me . . . *(Weeps and throws herself on his neck)*

YASHA

Why cry? *(Drinks champagne)* In six days I'll be back in Paris. Tomorrow we'll get on the express and go rolling off, and that's the last you'll see of us. I can hardly believe it. Veev la France! . . . I can't live here, it's not for me . . . that's how it is. I've had enough of looking at this ignorance. *(Drinks champagne)* Why cry? If you behaved yourself properly, you wouldn't cry.

DUNYASHA

(Looks in a small mirror and powders her nose) Send me a letter from Paris. I loved you, Yasha, I loved you so! I'm a pampered creature, Yasha!

YASHA

They're coming. *(Busies himself with the suitcases, humming softly)*

Lyubov Andreevna, Gaev, Anya and Charlotta Ivanovna enter.

GAEV

We ought to go. There's not much time left. *(Looking at Yasha)* Who smells of herring?

LYUBOV ANDREEVNA

In about ten minutes let's get into the carriages . . . *(Gazes around the room)* Good-bye, dear house, old grandfather. Winter will pass, spring will come, and you'll be no more, you'll be torn down. These walls have seen so much! *(Kisses her daughter warmly)* You're beaming, my treasure, your dear eyes are sparkling like two diamonds. So you're glad? Very glad?

ANYA

Very! It's the beginning of a new life, mama!

GAEV

(Cheerfully) In fact, all's well now. Before the sale of the cherry orchard, we were all upset, we suffered, but once the question was

decided finally, irrevocably, we all calmed down, became cheerful even . . . I'm a bank official now, a financier . . . yellow into the side . . . and you, Lyuba, are looking better, after all, no doubt about it.

LYUBOV ANDREEVNA

Yes. My nerves are better, it's true.

She is given her hat and coat.

I sleep well. Carry my things out, Yasha. It's time. *(To Anya)* My dear girl, we'll see each other soon . . . I'm going to Paris, I'll live there on the money your great-aunt from Yaroslavl sent to buy the estate—long live our great-aunt!—and that money won't last long.

ANYA

You'll come back soon, mama, very soon . . . won't you? I'll study, pass the exams at school, and then I'll work, I'll help you. We'll read all kinds of books together, mama . . . Won't we? *(Kisses her mother's hands)* We'll read in the autumn evenings, we'll read lots of books, and a new, wonderful world will open before us . . . *(Dreamily)* Come back, mama . . .

LYUBOV ANDREEVNA

I will, my jewel. *(Embraces Anya)*

Lopakhin enters. Charlotta softly hums a little song.

GAEV

Happy Charlotta: she's singing!

CHARLOTTA

(Picks up a bundle which looks like a swaddled baby) Bye-o, baby, bye-o . . .

Sound of a baby crying: "Wah, wah!"

Hush, my sweet, my dear little boy.

"Wah! Wah!"

I'm so sorry for you! *(Throws the bundle back where it had been)* So, find me a position, please. I can't go on like this.

LOPAKHIN

We will, Charlotta Ivanovna, don't worry.

GAEV

Everybody's abandoning us, Varya's leaving . . . we've suddenly become unnecessary.

CHARLOTTA

I've got nowhere to live in town . . . I have to leave . . . *(Hums)* Who cares . . .

Pishchik enters.

LOPAKHIN

A wonder of nature! . . .

PISHCHIK

(Breathless) Oh, let me catch my breath . . . I'm worn out . . . My esteemed friends . . . Give me some water . . .

GAEV

In need of money, no doubt? Your humble servant, I'll get out of harm's way . . . *(Exits)*

PISHCHIK

Haven't been here for quite some time . . . most beautiful lady . . . *(To Lopakhin)* So you're here . . . glad to see you . . . a man of vast intellect . . . here . . . take this . . . *(Hands Lopakhin money)* Four hundred roubles . . . I still owe you eight hundred and forty . . .

LOPAKHIN

(Shrugs his shoulders in bewilderment) Am I dreaming? . . . Where'd you get it?

PISHCHIK

Wait . . . I'm hot . . . A most extraordinary event . . . Some Englishmen came to me and found some sort of white clay in my soil . . .
(To Lyubov Andreevna) Four hundred for you . . . my beautiful,
astonishing lady . . . *(Hands her the money)* The rest later. *(Drinks
water)* Just now a young man on the train was telling how some . . .
great philosopher supposedly recommends jumping off the roof . . .
"Jump!" he says. That's all there is to it. *(With surprise)* Imagine
that! Water! . . .

LOPAKHIN

Who are these Englishmen?

PISHCHIK

I leased them the plot with the clay for twenty-four years . . . And
now, forgive me, no time . . . I must gallop on . . . I'm going to
Znoikov . . . to Kardamonov . . . I owe them all . . . *(Drinks)* Be
well . . . I'll come by on Thursday . . .

LYUBOV ANDREEVNA

We're moving to town now, and tomorrow I'm going abroad . . .

PISHCHIK

What's that? *(Alarmed)* Why to town? Aha, I see, the furniture . . .
suitcases . . . Well, never mind . . . *(Through tears)* Never mind . . .
They're people of vast intelligence . . . these Englishmen . . . Never
mind . . . I wish you all happiness . . . God will help you . . . Never
mind . . . Everything in this world must come to an end . . . *(Kisses
Lyubov Andreevna's hand)* And when the news reaches you that
I've met my end, remember this old horse and say: "Once upon
a time there lived a . . . a . . . Simeonov-Pishchik . . . God rest his
soul" . . . Most wonderful weather . . . Yes . . . *(Exits in great confu-
sion, but comes back at once and says from the doorway)* Dashenka
sends her greetings! *(Exits)*

LYUBOV ANDREEVNA

Now we can go. I'm leaving with two worries. The first is the ailing Firs. *(Glancing at her watch)* Another five minutes . . .

ANYA

Firs has been sent to the hospital, mama. Yasha sent him this morning.

LYUBOV ANDREEVNA

My second grief is—Varya. She's used to getting up early and working, and now, without work, she's like a fish out of water. The poor thing's grown thin, pale, and she keeps crying . . .

Pause.

As you know very well, Ermolai Alexeich, I dreamed . . . of giving her away to you, and it did look as if you were going to marry her. *(Whispers to Anya, who nods to Charlotta, and both exit)* She loves you, you're fond of her, and I don't know, I don't know why it is that you seem to avoid each other. I don't understand!

LOPAKHIN

I admit, I don't understand it either. It's all somehow strange . . . If there's still time, I'm ready right now . . . Let's finish it at once—and be done! Because without you, I have a feeling I won't propose.

LYUBOV ANDREEVNA

Excellent. It will only take a minute. I'll call her at once . . .

LOPAKHIN

There's champagne, as it happens. *(Looks at the glasses)* They're empty. Somebody drank it all.

Yasha coughs.

That's what's known as slurping it up . . .

LYUBOV ANDREEVNA

(Animated) Wonderful. We'll step outside . . . Yasha, *allez!* I'll call her . . . *(Through the door)* Varya, drop everything and come here. Come! *(Exits with Yasha)*

LOPAKHIN

(Glancing at his watch) Hm, yes . . .

Pause.

   Restrained laughter and whispering behind the door; Varya finally enters.

VARYA

(Examining the luggage for a long time) Strange, I just can't find . . .

LOPAKHIN

What are you looking for?

VARYA

I packed it myself and now I don't remember.

Pause.

LOPAKHIN

Where will you be going now, Varvara Mikhailovna?

VARYA

Me? To the Ragulins' . . . We've arranged for me to look after their household . . . as housekeeper or something.

LOPAKHIN

In Yashnevo, isn't it? Some fifty miles from here.

Pause.

So life in this house is over . . .

VARYA

(Looking over the luggage) Where is that . . . Maybe I packed it in the trunk . . . Yes, life is over in this house . . . there won't be any more . . .

LOPAKHIN

And I'm about to leave for Kharkov . . . on this train. There's a lot to do. I'm leaving Epikhodov here . . . I've hired him.

VARYA

Well, then!

LOPAKHIN

Last year around this time it was already snowing, if you remember, and now it's calm and sunny. Only it's cold . . . Three below.

VARYA

I didn't look . . .

Pause.

Besides, our thermometer's broken . . .

Pause.
  Voice through the door from outside: "Ermolai Alexeich!"

LOPAKHIN

(As if he had long been waiting for that call) Coming! *(Quickly exits)*

Varya sits down on the floor, her head on a bundle of clothes, and softly weeps.
  The door opens, Lyubov Andreevna enters cautiously.

LYUBOV ANDREEVNA

Well?

Pause.

We must go.

VARYA

(No longer weeping, her tears wiped) Yes, it's time, mama. I'll hurry off to the Ragulins' today, if only I'm not late for the train . . .

LYUBOV ANDREEVNA

(Through the door) Anya, put your coat on!

Anya enters, then Gaev and Charlotta Ivanovna. Gaev is wearing a warm coat with a hood. Servants and coachmen gather. Epikhodov busies himself with the luggage.

Now we can be on our way.

ANYA

(Joyfully) On our way!

GAEV

My friends, my dear, good friends! In leaving this house forever, how can I be silent, how can I keep from expressing, by way of farewell, the feelings that now fill my whole being . . .

ANYA

(Entreating) Oh, uncle!

VARYA

Dearest uncle, don't!

GAEV

(Dejectedly) Double the yellow into the side . . . I'll be quiet . . .

Trofimov enters, then Lopakhin.

TROFIMOV

Well, ladies and gentlemen, it's time to go!

187

LOPAKHIN

Epikhodov, my coat!

LYUBOV ANDREEVNA

I'll sit down for one little minute more. It's as if I never saw before what sort of walls this house has, what sort of ceilings, and now I look at them greedily, with such tender love . . .

GAEV

I remember when I was six years old, sitting in this window at Pentecost and watching my father walk to church . . .

LYUBOV ANDREEVNA

Has all the luggage been taken out?

LOPAKHIN

It seems so. *(To Epikhodov, putting on his coat)* Epikhodov, see that everything's in order.

EPIKHODOV

(Speaking in a husky voice) Don't you worry, Ermolai Alexeich!

LOPAKHIN

What's wrong with your voice?

EPIKHODOV

I just took a drink of water and swallowed something.

YASHA

(Contemptuously) Ignorance . . .

LYUBOV ANDREEVNA

We'll leave—and there won't be a soul left here . . .

LOPAKHIN

Till spring.

VARYA

(Pulls an umbrella from a bundle, looks as if she's raising it to hit him; Lopakhin pretends to be frightened) Don't worry, don't worry . . . I wasn't going to . . .

TROFIMOV

Let's get into the carriages, ladies and gentlemen . . . It's time! The train's about to come!

VARYA

Here are your galoshes, Petya, next to this suitcase. *(In tears)* They're so dirty, so old . . .

TROFIMOV

(Putting on his galoshes) Let's go, ladies and gentlemen!

GAEV

(Very confused, afraid he will start weeping) The train . . . the station . . . *Croisé* into the side . . . double the white into the corner . . .

LYUBOV ANDREEVNA

Let's go!

LOPAKHIN

Everybody here? Nobody in there? *(Locks the side door to the left)* Things have been put in storage there, it's got to be locked up. Let's go! . . .

ANYA

Good-bye, house! Good-bye, old life!

TROFIMOV

Hello, new life! . . . *(Exits with Anya)*

Varya looks around the room and exits unhurriedly. Exit Yasha and Charlotta with her little dog.

189

LOPAKHIN

Till spring, then. Step out, ladies and gentlemen . . . Bye-bye! . . .
(Exits)

Lyubov Andreevna and Gaev remain alone. As if they had been waiting for it, they throw themselves on each other's necks and weep restrainedly, softly, for fear of being heard.

GAEV

(In despair) My sister, my sister . . .

LYUBOV ANDREEVNA

Oh, my dear, my tender, my beautiful orchard! . . . My life, my youth, my happiness, good-bye! . . . Good-bye! . . .

Anya's voice calling cheerfully: "Mama! . . ." Trofimov's voice cheerfully, excitedly: "Yoo-hoo! . . ."

One last look at these walls, these windows . . . Our late mother liked to walk about in this room . . .

GAEV

My sister, my sister! . . .

Anya's voice: "Mama! . . ." Trofimov's voice: "Yoo-hoo!"

LYUBOV ANDREEVNA

We're coming! . . .

They exit.

The stage is empty. There is the sound of keys turning in all the doors, then of the carriages driving off. Then all is quiet. Amidst the quiet there is the muted noise of an axe striking wood, sounding solitary and sad. Footsteps are heard. From the door to the right, Firs appears. He is dressed as usual in a jacket and white waistcoat, with slippers on his feet. He is ill.

FIRS

(Goes to the door, tries the handle) Locked. They've gone . . . *(Sits down on the sofa)* Forgot about me . . . Never mind . . . I'll sit here for a bit . . . Leonid Andreich probably didn't put on his fur coat, went just in his topcoat . . . *(Preoccupied sigh)* I didn't check on him . . . Green youth! *(Mutters something incomprehensible)* Life's gone by, as if I never lived. *(Lies down)* I'll lie down for a bit . . . You've got no strength, you've got nothing left, nothing . . . Eh, you . . . blunderhead! . . . *(Lies still)*

A distant sound, as if from the sky, the sound of a breaking string, dying away, sad. Silence ensues, and the only thing heard is an axe striking wood far off in the orchard.

    Curtain.

Anton Pavlovich Chekhov (1860–1904) was born in Taganrog, on the Sea of Azov. His grandfather was a serf, but managed to buy his freedom and that of his family some years before the abolition of serfdom by the emperor Alexander II in 1861. Chekhov attended the Greek high school in Taganrog, and, on graduating in 1879, went on to study medicine in Moscow. In that same year he wrote his first play, entitled *Fatherlessness* and later known as *Platonov*, after the central character. It was never published or performed in his lifetime, but has recently been produced to great acclaim. To support himself in medical school, Chekhov wrote comic sketches for the newspapers, as he had done earlier in Taganrog, but by the time he graduated in 1884, writing had become a more serious matter for him. In that same year he first showed symptoms of the tuberculosis that was to cut short his life. In 1887 a theater director in Moscow commissioned a play from him, and ten days later Chekhov gave him *Ivanov*, which was produced with success in Moscow and a year later in Petersburg. He also wrote a number of one-act comic sketches during those years. Then in 1894 he wrote *The Seagull*, the first of the four great plays that have since become central works of modern theater. The original production, in Petersburg, was disappointing, especially for Chekhov, but the play was noticed by Vladimir Nemirovich-Danchenko, co-founder with Konstantin Stanislavsky of the new Moscow Art Theatre. Their production in 1898 was a triumph and is now recognized as one of the greatest events in Russian, and world, theater. Chekhov's next play, *Uncle Vanya*, was published in 1897 and produced by the Moscow Art Theatre in 1899. It was followed by *Three Sisters* in 1901 and, finally, by *The Cherry Orchard* in 1904.

During the spring of that year, Chekhov's tuberculosis became critical; he went to a sanatorium in Badenweiler, in the Black Forest, and died there in mid-July.

RICHARD NELSON's plays include the four-play series *The Apple Family: Scenes from Life in the Country* (*That Hopey Changey Thing*, *Sweet and Sad*, *Sorry* and *Regular Singing*), *Nikolai and the Others*, *Farewell to the Theatre*, *Conversations in Tusculum*, *How Shakespeare Won the West*, *Frank's Home*, *Rodney's Wife*, *Franny's Way*, *Madame Melville*, *Goodnight Children Everywhere*, *New England*, *The General from America*, *Misha's Party* (with Alexander Gelman), *Two Shakespearean Actors* and *Some Americans Abroad*. He has written the musicals *James Joyce's The Dead* (with Shaun Davey) and *My Life with Albertine* (with Ricky Ian Gordon), and the screenplays for the films *Hyde Park-on-Hudson* and *Ethan Frome*. He has received numerous awards, including a Tony (Best Book of a Musical for *James Joyce's The Dead*), an Olivier (Best Play for *Goodnight Children Everywhere*) and two New York Drama Critics' Circle Awards (*James Joyce's The Dead* and *The Apple Family*). He is the recipient of the PEN/Laura Pels Master Playwright Award, an Academy Award from the American Academy of Arts and Letters; he is an Honorary Associate Artist of the Royal Shakespeare Company. He lives in upstate New York.

RICHARD PEVEAR was born in Boston, grew up on Long Island, attended Allegheny College (BA 1964) and the University of Virginia (MA 1965). After a stint as a college teacher, he moved to the Maine coast and eventually to New York City, where he worked as a freelance writer, editor and translator, and also as a cabinetmaker. He has published two collections of poetry, many essays and reviews, and some thirty books translated from French, Italian and Russian.

LARISSA VOLOKHONSKY was born in Leningrad, attended Leningrad State University and, on graduating, joined a scientific team whose work took her to the far east of Russia, to Kamchatka and

Sakhalin Island. She emigrated to Israel in 1973, and to the United States in 1975, where she attended Yale Divinity School and St. Vladimir's Theological Seminary. Soon after settling in New York City, she married Richard Pevear, and a few years later they moved to France with their two children.

Together, Pevear and Volokhonsky have translated twenty books from the Russian, including works by Fyodor Dostoevsky, Leo Tolstoy, Mikhail Bulgakov, Anton Chekhov, Boris Pasternak and Nikolai Leskov. Their translation of Dostoevsky's *The Brothers Karamazov* received the PEN Translation Prize for 1991; their translation of Tolstoy's *Anna Karenina* was awarded the same prize in 2002; and in 2006 they were awarded the first Efim Etkind International Translation Prize by the European University of St. Petersburg.